JOHN LYMINGTON

THE VALE OF SAD BANANA

Complete and Unabridged

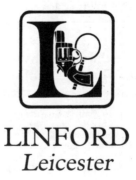

LINFORD
Leicester

First published in Great Britain in 1984 by
Robert Hale Limited
London

First Linford Edition
published 2003
by arrangement with
Robert Hale Limited
London

British Library CIP Data

Lymington, John, *1911 – 1983*
    The Vale of Sad Banana.—Large print ed.—
Linford mystery library
    1. Detective and mystery stories
    2. Large type books
    I. Title
    823.9'12 [F]

    ISBN 0–7089–9442–3

Published by
F. A. Thorpe (Publishing)
Anstey, Leicestershire

Set by Words & Graphics Ltd.
Anstey, Leicestershire
Printed and bound in Great Britain by
T. J. International Ltd., Padstow, Cornwall

This book is printed on acid-free paper

1

1

The summer that the world ended began in April, cutting short the joyous changes of weather with a succession of dry, hot, cloudless days that was unusual for that time of year. And the hot, cloudless days went on, through May to June when the first Unseen Disaster happened far out in the boundless blue. Each morning began with a varicoloured heat haze that shimmered over the village and the fields, made ghosts of the trees in Bell Wood and painted shifting mirages above the almost still, dwindling river. Then suddenly the haze of pearly pink vanished and the dry bright summer sun burnt steadily until night, when the heat of it still lingered, folding on the skin like a loose blanket one couldn't kick off. And in the morning the pearly haze of shifting colours came again for another day the same as the last, and the last before that, and the last before that, till nobody could remember the day it had begun.

At eight on the morning of 14 June, Jeff Wise, landlord of The Bygone Arms, came out of the front door of his pub and looked across his dusty car-park and the road to the haze on the meadows. Far off, the trees of Bell Wood showed like bushes floating on the mist. The day smelt fine and fresh but soon it would be hot again, and dry.

'This,' said Wise, 'is beginning to get boring.' For a moment he felt as if he had cursed a god who would strike him down. It passed. He sat down on the oak bench against the pub wall. He looked at his dog lying in the dust, flat as a thick red rug, then watched two young thrushes kicking up a dust-bath in a hollow where the puddles used to be. He wondered why they did that. One day, perhaps, he would ask, or perhaps he would prefer to keep wondering.

'I must get this car-park tarmacked,' he said aloud. 'The dust is coming in the bar, what with the doors open all the time.' The dog wagged his tail twice, thumping the dust, then sat up suddenly and warned off a fly which settled on his tail. 'How the hell does he feel a fly with all that hair?' The dog lay flat again. Jeff Wise had almost forgotten what it was like to have hair. He had balded early. Redheads do, they told him. Now when it rained it was like somebody playing a kettledrum on his head. When it rained . . . Ah, when it rained . . .

His wife called out through the open door: 'What're you doin', Jeff?'

'Sittin',' he said, leaning his back against the wall. He listened to his wife call out a list of things that needed doing. 'Sounds like a tape goin' backwards,' he thought, and watched the thrushes fly off over the hedge and into the ash tree.

The mail van came round the corner, and turned into the car-park. Engines all sounded noisy in the heat, Jeff thought, and was relieved when Jim switched it off. He must be going potty getting needled by a thing like that, Jeff thought, but this heat . . .

'It's bloody hot,' the postman said,

coming up and sitting beside Jeff. 'I'm beginning to feel wary. You know what I mean?'

'You mean you're waiting for the thunderstorm to end all thunderstorms,' Jeff said.

'Well, it is unusual, you'll admit.' He rested his back against the wall. 'Indians say the world's going to end on Sunday.'

'They often do,' said Jeff. 'It's what they do instead of forecasting football results.'

'Still, you know, somebody gets it right now and again.'

'If they get *this* right, there ain't going to be an again,' said Jeff, and laughed. 'You're gettin' heat blues, mate. Used to get it in the desert. A long time ago — when I had hair to stop my hat sliding about.'

'I had post for Old Will's cottage yesterday, and Monday,' Jim said. 'Beautiful couple of women. Lovely. Reminds me of everything I ever stood for.'

'Sir Hugh's daughters, I thought you'd given up women.'

'I'd make an exception. They were

4

having a row though, yesterday. You could feel it. Like an electric belt round the cottage.'

'An electric belt!' Jeff gave a contemptuous chuckle. 'You're like the women in this village. Fey. The things that get felt round here aren't all fleshy. I reckon we've got six witches, by local count. Don't you start up as well.'

'I could feel it, Jeff. It was an atmosphere.'

Witches, Jeff thought. Flo Brett, big old solid Flo who could tell fortunes in tea-leaves and read peoples' palms; little skinny, elbows-in Miss Wainwright, who hopped and scuttled like a mouse but played cards with herself and talked while she did it, and then got strange messages from God knows where; and Bet Hicks — ah, Bet! She was a different kind of witch. She could cure things and make people happy with herbs or make people happier by being Bet Hicks. He smiled a moment then rubbed his back against the wall.

'It's too bloody hot,' the postman said, and yawned. 'I got worn out not sleeping proper because of the heat and took one of the wife's pills last night. Can't bloody wake up now.'

Jeff looked askance at him.

'Sleeping-pill? Oh.' He nodded.

'Why? Something wrong with that?'

'Not if they suit you. That sort of thing don't suit me. I get hazy all day.' He laughed and stood up.

'Come in and have a cuppa tea.'

'No, ta. Too hot.'

'No, no, no, lad. Hot tea cools you down. It makes your skin hot so all the hot air rushes up through your clothes and out your collar and the cold air rushes in up your trousers and in no time at all you're got frozen balls.' The landlord laughed heartily then.

'You're in a good mood this mornin', Jeff,' the postman said.

'No. Not yet. But I reckon if you come in for a cuppa, the lady wife won't have the chance to bawl at me and I can eat in peace.' He heaved himself up from the seat.

The dog slapped the ground twice with his tail, then was still again. The morning droned with the heat.

When the postman came out again, the dog slapped the ground once.

'What's the matter with you, Flag? Sleepy sickness? You usually get up for me.' He watched the dog raise his head, look at him, flap his tail, then sink into repose again. 'Perhaps it's an omen. Animals always know when something's going to happen.'

He laughed as he got into the van, but, all the same, he felt it was a funny kind of morning and couldn't think why.

Jeff sat eating eggs and fat bacon. His wife was at the open larder door counting provisions.

'I was woke up sudden — marmalade,' she said, without turning round.

'Right,' Jeff said. 'You were woke up sudden with marmalade.'

'Not with marmalade,' she snapped, making a little clatter with a mechanical shopping indicator. 'I was woke up sudden in the night. I sat up. I thought something had fallen. A picture. They're unlucky. Pictures. Rice. I got up and came down to look, but there wasn't nothing out of place.'

'It didn't wake me,' he said. 'What time was this?'

'Just after three. You was deep in. I didn't disturb you. It gave me a funny feeling. I thought something dreadful had happened, but couldn't find anything. You know?' She turned round then.

'Yes, I know. It's three-o'clock-in-the-morning blues. The body entrails is at the lowest heat. Lots of folk wake up and die at that time. Very popular for panic is three o'clock.' He frowned over buttering toast. 'Come to think — I had funny kind of dream. What the hell was it? I woke in a bit of a sweat. Not heat. Fright. I got out of bed because I couldn't get it out of my head. It was sort of chasing me, every time I shut my eyes to try and sleep again . . .'

'What was? Something you were dreaming about?'

'No, I think it was just the horrible thought of what had been in the dream. I actually got up before I realized I was really awake, and then I was relieved . . . But I can't bloody remember what

8

the dream was about!'

'Perhaps you heard the noise in your sleep,' she said. 'I'm sure I heard something. I've been looking all round this morning again, but I can't see anything.'

'Was it Flag making a noise?'

'No. I couldn't find him. Do you know where he was? Out in the kennel.'

'The kennel? Only owls ever goes in there! He never does.'

'Well, he came out of it last night when I whistled, but he turned round and went back in it again.'

Jeff sat back, the uneasiness of the night returning.

'It's this blasted heat,' he said.

His wife went away upstairs. He went on consulting the racing pages of the morning paper.

She came down dressed and tidied. 'I meant to ask; why were you outside so long with Jim Brett last night? Talking and talking out there.'

'I was dissuading,' Jeff said. 'I knew there was something up when he sat there in the corner all evening sharpening that knife. He had a bit of stone in his pocket. Nasty-looking knife, too. Every time he had another beer he sharpened it faster. So when he went I felt my duty was to stop him doing whatever he had in mind — what there is of it.'

'Did he tell you what?'

'He did in the end, yes.'

'What did he want to do? Kill somebody?'

'No. He wanted to cut the colonel's balls off.'

'He couldn't have been serious.'

'He bloody was. That's why I took so long talking him out of it. I got him to leave the knife behind.'

'What had the colonel done?' she asked very curiously.

'I couldn't get him to say. He kept saying, 'No need for you to mind.' Anyhow, in the end I told him they'd shut him up in a loony-bin for the rest of his natural if he tried to do anything like that, and the idea of that finally got through. I ought to have taken on a diplomat's career. I wouldn't have made a mess of it as often as they do.'

'It's all part of the service, helping the customer,' she said. 'But I think Brett ought to be put away anyhow.'

She went.

Jeff washed up his breakfast things, tidied the table, then took his morning paper out to the front, once again sat on the bench, and turned to the reports of world affairs.

After a while of 'seeing through' the wiles of international politicians, Jeff saw Bobby Miller come up on his bike. The boy dismounted, stood the bike in a lean-to attitude, bent down and fussed the dog.

'Hallo, Mr Wise. Pretty morning again,' the boy said, crouching as he fussed the dog's head. 'I've brought the herbs for Mrs Wise, from home.' He straightened, took the paper cone of greenstuff from his bike bag and carried it to Jeff. The dog got up and followed him.

The boy laid the package on the seat and sat down by it. The dog put his head between his legs to have it fussed some more.

'And how is Mrs Hicks?' Jeff said.

'She sends her love — but not if Mrs Wise is in,' the boy said, almost in a whisper. He grinned.

'Saucy bugger,' Jeff said, and laughed. 'And what wonders of the world have you been reading about this week, then?'

'A book,' Bobby said. 'And it says that the whole of the universe — all the stars, planets, constellations and all of it are only the atoms in the boot heel of a giant.'

'I have heard of it,' Jeff said. 'It's meant to stop you getting big ideas. Not you, boy. Everybody.'

'Suppose it's true,' said Bobby, eagerly. 'Then one day the boot wears out, and what then?'

'The universe gets smaller?' said Jeff, raising his eyebrows.

'Suppose he doesn't want worn boots,' the boy said, bright eyed. 'Suppose he's seen a new pair he wants. Then what?'

'Well, what?'

'He throws the old boot on the bonfire!' said Bobby, almost in triumph.

Jeff sat back against the wall and ran a

handkerchief round the inside of his collar.

'Bonfire, damn it! It's too hot to think of bonfires as well.' He was going to say, 'Makes you think we're on a bloody bonfire now!', but he felt it somehow unwise. 'What on earth made you think of that?'

'Well, you spray poison for flies and try and kill everything that's small and a nuisance so why shouldn't the giant do it, too? I mean, we're no more important than a wasp or a beetle.'

'We are, boy,' Jeff said, uneasily.

'But who said so?' said Bobby, curiously. 'Only men.'

Jeff felt he should say, 'God said so,' but he didn't believe God ever did say so. He never liked thinking about such things in the morning. Specially not when it was hot.

'You've got all this week off, have you? When I was at school we only had just the day, not the whole ruddy week. I wouldn't mind being a teacher nowadays.'

'What would you teach, Mr Wise?'

'Hotel management,' said Jeff, and felt

better. 'What are you planning to do today?'

'I don't know. I'll go and see Dr Ritchie later. He was sad yesterday.'

'What about?'

'He was dressed up in his kilt and sporran and frilly shirt and that always makes him sad. He cried yesterday.'

'Boozer's gloom,' thought Jeff. 'A case of Scotch a week's enough to gloom any boozer, I'd say.'

'He played the bagpipes,' said Bobby, with a strange delight at the oddity.

'Christ,' said Jeff, beneath his breath. 'What was he sad about?'

'He thinks about Scotland, then he's sad. But I think he just likes to have a cry. Liz says the bagpipes would make anybody cry. I don't like 'em much because they moan all the time.'

'He's a very clever man, they say.'

'Oh yes, he is! He designs space vehicles — or parts of them, he says. Only parts, he always says. He's always putting me right, then laughing, so I don't really know if he's serious or not. He made a joke about the Indians when he stopped crying. He said he felt it was the end of the world that made him cry and the Indians said it would be Sunday.'

Jeff almost started. It was the second time that morning he had heard the same news, yet he had not seen anything of it in the papers. Perhaps he had missed it.

'Sunday, is it?' Jeff said, rather blankly.

'No,' said Bobby, firmly. 'It won't be this week at all.'

Jeff looked at him very curiously.

'And how do *you* know?' he said.

'I don't know,' the boy said. 'But it won't be Sunday.'

He pushed the dog away and got up. 'I must get on. Goodbye, Mr Wise.'

'Thanks for the herbs, tell her,' Jeff called after him. He watched the cyclist ride away. 'Strange boy,' he told the dog. 'The way he says things. Some things. As if he knows!' He chuckled and went on reading his paper, but stopped again and looked at the bunch of herbs.

The boy always called her Liz, not Bet, like everybody else. But it was difficult for him to know what to call her. She was his grandmother, or was she? It had been a mystery for years, although it had happened right under the nose of the village. Even now, so long after, nobody had quite decided the truth of the matter. Of course she was an extraordinary woman, but hadn't it been just a bit too extraordinary? And what had happened to the daughter? Where had she gone that she had never been heard of again? It was odd. One would have thought the oddness would have worn away by now, but somehow it stayed. And perhaps extraordinary people were odd anyway . . .

He turned to his paper again until he heard the soft whirring of the bike again and looked up. The boy rode up, then began to circle extremely slowly as if daring the bike to fall over.

'Did you wake up in the night?' Bobby said, watching the ground.

'Why?' Jeff had a sudden catch somewhere in his stomach and felt a small anger about it.

'We did. I woke up. I thought I heard a big bang in the sky, so I got up and looked out and Liz was standing down by

16

the river in the moonlight. It looked all magical — but the river's getting low. Sad, that is. Sort of dying.'

'Was there a bang?' Jeff said, watching the boy staring at the dust under the silent wheels.

'No. Liz says there wasn't at all, but she said she got up before because she felt funny. Sort of anxious, she said. So she went down the garden to the river. She feels peaceful there, only last night she didn't. She said she felt something happened. So she made some tea and went back to bed.'

'Mrs Wise woke up,' Jeff said. 'She said same as you. Thought there was a bang.'

'I know what it was now,' Bobby said, bracing his legs to strike out fast.

'What?'

'The bonfire's starting to crackle!' shouted Bobby, then sped away as Jeff threw his folded paper at him.

The dog barked and, forgetting the heat, ran after the speeding boy. Jeff got up to retrieve his paper and thought about Bet standing by the silent river in the moonlight.

So she had known before it happened. What happened? Nothing happened. They all knew nothing happened . . . But yes; something did happen. They all woke up about three. That's what happened. He didn't wake up but he dreamed and felt the same when he woke up — that something had happened and frightened him. Everybody knew something happened but nobody heard anything, nobody saw anything, nobody felt anything . . . But yes, they did feel something. But it wasn't that kind of feeling, like feeling a bang or an earthquake. Nothing like that at all. No. A feeling inside that you *knew* something happened.

But Bet had known something was *going to* happen. That was the difference. That was how Bet was different. That was why some people thought she was a witch. She knew things other people didn't. She could do things other people couldn't.

He turned, shut and locked the door, pocketed the key and walked slowly down the village to the bakery to the woman who shared his extra private life.

* * *

Annie Bettys was fat, 33, very fair with peaches and cream skin, blue eyes and a sparkling sort of laugh. Jeff Wise loved her, and, from time to time, she loved him. Mrs Wise knew there was something, but had long rested almost content in the calculation that with two such fat bellies nothing could happen of any importance.

Jeff turned up the side alley to the half door of the bakery behind the shop. The smell of fresh baked bread still lingered on the morning air.

Annie was in the bakehouse, still in her white wrap-round overall.

She looked up from making entries in her order book.

'Why, 'tis Jeff, the wisest, fattest, of them all,' she said. 'Funny time of day for you.'

'Restless,' he said.

'Thanks.'

'Slept badly. Put me on edge. Maud woke about three and started marching round the house. Thought she'd heard a picture fall down.'

'About three?' Annie's blue eyes became very keen. 'Funny that. There was something in the night, but I really don't know what.'

'What something do you mean?'

'I'd just put the first batch in the oven — just before three. I didn't get my usual four hours. Woke up about half two and got up rather than drop off again. You know, if you drop off at get-up time you really drop. I came down and got things ready — it was all ready, but I always have a last look round. Well, I put the batch in. It was some hot, I tell you, but I'm well used to that. Then quite suddenly I had a sort of small panic. I don't know whether I got the idea the oven would blow up, or the roof fall in on me, but I just had to get outside. You know that sort of panic when you dream you can't breathe? Well, I went out into the alley and looked up, and I do remember having some weird idea I was looking to make sure the sky was still up there. By a coincidence, it was, but something . . . '

She stopped and looked as if she couldn't find the word.

'Was there a bang? Maud said — '

'No. Not a bang. It was worse. It was absolute silence. I've never heard such a silence in my life. That's absurd. Of course I didn't hear it. It was a sensation — like falling a great distance in nothing at all. You dream you're going to stub your toe on a kerb and your whole inside stops dead. Like that.'

He leant on the half door, saying nothing, watching her, tense for her to go on.

'It lasted only a few seconds. That's all. But when it was over, there was no feeling of relief. Maud's right. There was a feeling that something had happened, but I couldn't find anything wrong. Of course I checked everything. I ended up using the mirror to test the whites of my eyes and the colour of my tongue. Strong disbeliever in anything supernatural that I don't like, I even took a couple of aspirins. It made no difference. And I'm still uneasy about it this morning.'

'It could have been something like an earthquake down the Pacific Crack,' he said, but thought, 'Everybody looked at the sky. They know it happened there.'

'Maybe. And maybe we think in terms of Rustum Magna in our modest little way,' she said. 'But supposing the whole world had it, at morning, noon, evening or night, all at the same time wherever they were, somebody will have to explain what it was, because it'll be *news*.'

'That should be interesting,' Jeff said. 'Every time anybody explains anything these days, some other geezer says the opposite. Should be worth a few weeks' arguing on the box.'

She looked at him very straight.

'You were worried, Jeff. How come?'

2

Bobby leant the bike against the wall of the tithe barn and went in at the big doors, which stood open. He hadn't seen them open since Dr Ritchie came. They were big, faded brown oak doors, towering into the sky. To stand between them was like being in a cathedral. He stood there for a minute or more, excited by watching the huge doors reaching to the sky as if they propped it up.

Inside the barn the east end had been divided from the main space by portable metal partitions, hiding Ritchie's machinery and electronic equipment.

When Bobby went in that day the doctor wasn't in his work place. He was sitting on one of the old hay platforms, still in his kilt but no sporran; the ruffled shirt half undone, his red hair dishevelled. He sat there staring at the brown brick floor, legs apart, holding a squat glass of whisky between them.

'What's the matter, Dr Ritchie?' Bobby said, frowning with curiosity more than concern.

Bobby had seen him sitting on the hay floor many times, a glass between his knees, thinking. But the boy could feel this morning was different.

'Matter?' said Ritchie, looking up with a terrible green eyed frown. His voice boomed like Big Ben. 'Nothing's the matter with *me*. But last night I saw the hand of God Almighty reach out and say, 'Hold!' and I am filled with awe.'

'You saw God in here?' said Bobby, looking up into the vast trusses of the roof.

'Correct: the hand of the Almighty in person.'

'What happened, sir?' The boy was excited, awed.

'At two hours, two minutes, thirty-eight point a million seconds, the world stopped and stayed stopped for three point two-seven-three-seven seconds. Stopped, boy. Came to a bloody standstill.'

'You mean stopped spinning?' Bobby's jaw was almost off its hinges.

'One must presume so. It is recorded on the computer watch, and I was here myself. I have verified it by phoning all over the world, boy. The system stopped. We're all very fortunate it went on again.'

He drank off his Scotch.

'But how?' said Bobby, eagerly. 'How could it stop?'

'Christ knows,' Ritchie said.

'Remember what you told me about the giant's boot heel?'

Ritchie laughed. 'You're not thinking the poor old giant's got gout, are you?'

'No. I think the boot's worn out and he's chucked it on the bonfire.'

Ritchie stared, then he laughed. He held out his glass.

'Fetch a dram for a starving Scot,' he said. 'You're scattier than I am, Robbie. But this I say; if it could all stop and us not fall off, then the sun must stop as well. The whole bloody issue must have stopped!'

A swallow came in through the great doors, swept round above the boy's head and fled again, crying out to draw the human's attention from the nest up in a beam above the doors.

'They'll be showing heads soon,' said Bobby. 'Do you know they fly right up from Africa? How do they find that nest every year?'

'Because they've left off where we haven't started yet,' Ritchie said, getting up. 'Get two blocks of milk chocolate from the shop, laddie. Here comes the master of the Rolls.'

The boy went out. A Rolls pulled up near his bike. Sir Hugh Rawley put his head out of the driver's window.

'Hallo, Bobby! Are you going home?'

'I can.'

'Ask Bet if she'd mind I called in this morning? About half an hour, say?'

'Of course, sir!' The boy leapt on the bike and pedalled away.

Sir Hugh got out of the car and went into the barn.

'Good God! Great Chieftain o' the Pudden-headed Race!' he said, taking the doctor's arm. 'Into the sanctum. This'll make your kilt fall down.'

They went through a door in the steel partition into a small room with a desk and phones, a table, chairs and a lot of papers everywhere. With no ceiling but the roof in the vasty shadows above, it looked like a film set.

'You look bad. Take a dram.'

'Not at half-past nine in the morning. We're flying down to London midday. There's an important meeting at three. Do you know what about? Put the bottle down! This'll be anaesthetic enough, I promise.'

'I obey. I wiggle my ears. What?'

'They've lost the Snark!'

'Lost it? What do you mean?'

'It's somewhere out there. Roaming!' Sir Hugh pointed to the roof beams. 'They have lost contact. It doesn't answer. That wonderful system of yours whereby the computer in it rejects any searching beams or rays or radar or Auntie Elsie's binoculars has rejected Control so now nobody knows where it is.'

He watched Ritchie's reaction. The reaction was standard as applied to all Ritchie's problems; he took a small dram.

'It's my computer system, you suggest,' he said. 'But you forget, what they wanted was a computer that could as near think as any computer could. I jigged one up. Your boys at the factory checked everything; made four prototypes, tested, retested, did everything. It went on to the ministry, was tested again, retested, given fourteen trials, test shots; it was installed in cars and left to drive in traffic . . . Surely there's no way that the thing could be faulty now?'

'The facts show it is. The Snark is lost.'

'You wanted a device that would prevent any form of detection, but could still be in touch with the operator, and that's what you've got. A computer that nearly thinks.'

'The trouble, dear boy, is that it *does* bloody well think!' said Sir Hugh angrily. 'It went off twenty hours ago on a patrol out there behind the Moon, and on the way that God-forsaken computer of yours suddenly thought, 'Bugger the human race', and it is switched off from Control and gone off on its own. The experts reckon that if it decides to stay on its original course it'll cruise round in space for maybe a couple of weeks and then come back and take a slice off the Moon. That will put the Diana's ear-ring out of balance. She'll wobble and our seas will come up and wash out the lot of us!'

'Small beer,' said Ritchie soberly. 'At two this morning, GMT, the whole bloody universe came to a halt. But if you insist on glory for the Snark, I'll get me pipes and play a lament.'

'Not with me here. Shave and clean up and be at my airstrip at half eleven. Right?'

'Have you still got a bar on board or shall I bring a wee bottle?'

Sir Hugh snorted, then, on his way to the door, stopped and wheeled round.

'The universe stopped?' he said, his eyes bulging at the slow-burnt thought. 'It couldn't have been Snark, could it?'

'Not unless that computer's got illusions of grandeur, Hugh. It's but a puny imp in the mighty matter of the universe. Less than a flea on a dog.'

'You agreed with the others it could upset the Moon, did you not?'

'Aye. I'd agree with me own murder to get away from a conference.'

'You don't believe it now?'

'Oh, I do believe it, but does it matter now that the universe has started having the urgles?'

Sir Hugh turned to the door. 'At the airstrip, then.'

'Ah toot ahloore,' said Ritchie, grinning. 'Let us take off soon! The earth's going to blow up!' He laughed.

★   ★   ★

'What do you want, Hugh?' Bet said. 'I've made some Darjeeling. In ten minutes I have work to do.'

Hugh grinned. 'Bet, my dear, I'm in trouble again.'

'Oh I am surprised,' she said quietly. 'Since you're always out hunting for the stuff, you mustn't get upset when you find it. Is this Another Thing that Might Happen?'

'In this case it seems sure to happen.'

'Your Mights always do seem sure to happen until afterwards. Tell me.'

He talked for twenty minutes over three cups of Darjeeling tea without milk. His soul was a little lightened. He kissed her hands and went away. She watched the Rolls go away.

'I must be a sponge,' she said.

They watched the village fall away under the windows. Ritchie sipped a straight malt and glared down thoughtfully.

'It's a wee place,' he said.

'It's smaller than that,' said Sir Hugh.

Up front the pilot said, 'Damn! I forgot to order the dog food. Now I'm going to worry. She kicks up hell if I don't get the twenty per-cent off.'

'Who? The dog?' said Hugh.

'Turn it upside down,' said Ritchie. 'The plane.'

'We'd fall through the roof,' said Hugh.

'That doesn't matter now, does it?' Ritchie said, and grinned.

'You're insane,' said Hugh.

'It *is* a small place,' said the pilot, nodding. 'Very small, really.'

'We've got the fate of the world in our hands,' said Ritchie and drank some more.

'No. I have,' said the pilot. 'If I say, we're all a mess of guts on the carpet.'

'I want to get out,' said Ritchie.

'Are you two trying to make me laugh?' shouted Hugh.

'It is a small place,' the pilot said, looking back and downwards. 'Very small.'

'Yet the people are the same size as in the big places,' said Ritchie. 'Very odd, that.'

'You don't care, do you!' Hugh hissed in his ear. 'You don't bloody well *care*!'

Ritchie stared across the great blue glass top to the flat little world of men. All their hopes, fears troubles and endeavours were locked up down there in the dark glass box. His troubles were all up here milling around in his head while he sat in a small aluminium cigar tube.

That sidereal pause. Could it have been the Snark hitting something out there? Hitting what? But what could have stopped the sun and its planets for whole seconds? Or were the instruments wrong? Had the machines recorded it wrong?

No. The whole lot recorded a stop. The cause couldn't have been Snark. It just could not.

But Snark had gone adrift. Was there a fault somewhere in the figures? Had the magic-headed boy got it wrong? He had never got it wrong before. He had been as good as the computers. Not now and again, but always. At times it looked as if the computers were following his instructions and giving his answers.

A cold hand gripped his heart.

Had they followed him?

He took another sip and laughed.

'What's funny?' said Hugh.

'I was considering possibilities and absurdities,' Ritchie said.

He sat deeper in his seat and looked out of the window again.

But could the boy have led them away? Was he some kind of magic-headed Pied Piper that all computers followed when he played?

'I have gone off my rails. I am floundering in manure,' he said half aloud.

'If you mean you're in the shit, you could be right,' said Hugh. 'But you're not alone, unfortunately.'

'The Snark couldn't do anything like last night,' said Ritchie, and to himself added, 'could it?'

He could not stop himself wondering

about Bobby Miller and the computers. And every time he did he scolded himself for foolishness. The boy had a magic gift, but he wasn't a bloody fairy who could change this, that or grandma's porridge with a touch of his magic finger —

Or was he? Science is a very odd subject; very surprising.

Every now and again a genius gets born. Strange things happen . . . But the boy had always been oddly gifted. Ritchie had been amused at first, as one is on finding the dog can play the piano. But suppose the dog goes on playing the piano, and you begin to realize he plays as well as anybody, and you listen to make sure it is good, and then begin to forget he's a dog . . . So with Bobby Miller. The boy's incredible capacity to juggle figures instantly in his head and produce the result at once was, at the start, rather funny. And then, like listening to the gifted dog, it had become less funny but rather acceptable, until in the end, due to its infallibility, it became a normal abnormality.

It had become easier to put the sum to

him than ask the computer. One didn't have to move a finger, but just check later. But when checked it was always right, so why go on checking?

Had he stopped checking on Bobby Miller? He couldn't remember. Had he come to think it a waste of time? That was impossible to remember.

Was Bobby Miller the trouble with Snark?

Again he laughed to himself. The countryside was ending below and the concrete sprawl was beginning, spreading like acid sludge on a clear pond. He hated it. He hated the mask of progress on a skull. He hated the science of prostituting nature. He hated computers. He hated the Snark. He hated —

No. He didn't hate Bobby Miller. None of it could be the boy's fault. It was his own fault. It was —

'Loop up your corsets,' said the pilot. 'We are about to strike dry land.'

Sir Hugh fastened his belt.

'We are going into a Bad Time,' he said.

'You tell me!' said Ritchie, and groaned. 'I think I'll get a doctor's certificate and get sent home.'

How the hell could Bobby Miller have been wrong, anyhow? After the job had left him the works had taken over, then the ministry, checking, double checking . . . No. It could be nothing to do with Bobby Miller.

He looked out of the window. They were on the tarmac. Doom lay just ahead.

He decided that, if he was not thrown into the Tower of London, he would go up to Scotland and visit his father, the laird. The laird had three young mistresses all of whom lived in the ramshackle castle and for all of whom the laird obtained tax relief by claiming one as a secretary, one as a nurse and one as housekeeper. Ritchie admired that. He wished he knew how so to handle bureaucracy that it diddled itself. He could use that sort of cunning right now.

2

1

Bobby Miller was an unusual boy. Children had always known it; adults were beginning to find out about it. There were some things Bobby Miller commented on that made people stop and feel uneasy, as if some familiar thing suddenly became frightening when he pointed it out.

But he had been unusual from the start, and that may have had something to do with his odd 'fey' comments. Bobby was unusual because Bet Hicks was unusual, as her father had been to put it mildly, unusually eccentric.

Tom Rogers had built boats at his cottage and workshop on the river bank. He had built very good boats, and when a squire from the next county came to him for his boats, Tom Rogers very graciously went to him for a wife. He selected the youngest daughter, Emmeline, and married her. As he could never abide her name, he called her Mudpatch. Their marriage was a riotous affair, which villagers thought so disgraceful that they hid in the woods behind the cottage by night to watch the revels of the happy pair and so collect evidence of this shameless saturnalia. The ecstatic cavortings were not confined to one wood, but were seen downriver in Bell Wood, where one or two regular accidental watchers noticed fairies joining in. The then rector, the Reverend Willums, a restful man, objected to a request for him to organise an exorcism of the woods.

'My dear Miss Grady,' he said, staring through eyebrow fringes, 'I cannot exorcise *Pan*! There would be nothing left for us to fight the good fight against. Besides, who can be sure which one of us would win such an exercise?'

But the observations of fairies on that site by the river was to be remembered years later.

Elizabeth was the first result of these private carnivals and was born while her mother was helping to hold together the hull of an unfinished boat.

'Tom, I'm going to have it!' — 'Just hold it one tick longer — just one tick — bugger! It's slipped.'

He then went to get his van out to fetch the doctor, but too late.

'Why didn't you say something?' he said, rushing to the boat birthplace with armfuls of blankets, bandages, gin and anything else he had thought handy in his scared haste. 'Christ! Is that it?'

'Well, what the hell do you think it is? Get a bowl of water and fetch Mrs Willow, then go for the doctor. I'm not going to build any more bloody boats!'

'Didn't you get any pains?' said the surprised doctor when he arrived.

'Of course. But they didn't seem bad enough.'

There were three more girls after Elizabeth.

'Cursed with women!' cried Tom. 'Not a boat builder in sight!'

Then disaster fell. Tom was devastated.

'If she'd died I would have got over it,' he said. 'If she'd run off with some other sod I'd have got over it. If she'd gone off to Antofagasta to dig for gold, I'd have got over it. If she'd gone off on a trip to Mars or bloody Utopia, I'd have got over it. But becoming a ruddy nun! A nun! After all that! A nun. It doesn't bear understanding. It's criminal lunacy. A nun! Religion! The nearest her family ever got to religion was to tip the parson to keep the sermon short. A nun! And all the time I was thinking she'd run off with a soap traveller!'

Perhaps there is a reason for everything, for one year after she had gone, Tom received a telegram from a convent in Devon asking him to come. He went, but his wife had died in the night.

'We prayed for her through the night,' Mother Superior said gently.

'It didn't do a lot of good,' he said, staring out of the window.

'We prayed for her soul,' the reverend lady explained.

There was a long silence.

'She's gone in search of a great perhaps,' Tom said, turning back to look at the saintly lady.

'Really!' she said, in the habit of reproof.

'It's not me who said it. A Frenchman said it when he was dying. I think he was a holy man, an abbé.'

'Who?' she frowned slightly.

'Rabelais,' Tom said. 'I'll make the arrangements.'

He drove to Land's End and stood looking from the clifftop at the rocks in a raging grey sea. The wind was hard. Flecks of spindrift sped past him as he looked into the great distance and cried until he was empty, then he got back into the car and drove the many miles to home and all the way tried to find the words he would use to tell the girls.

He brought up his four daughters with great humour and quiet strength, though it was some years before he began to realize that what he was suggesting for them was what they'd put into his head. A man in a minority of one to four daughters is lucky in that he only has to pretend to make his own decisions.

One summer day, when Elizabeth Hicks was 17, Christopher Hicks, a

Foreign correspondent resting from a shot leg, spent an hour's break from motoring through by walking in Bell Wood to relieve the pain from his wound.

He sat on a rock by the side of the river. It was on the edge of the wood. To his left, through a thin belt of trees, he saw the ground break out into a wide meadow. A young couple sauntered towards him on the towpath, at its edge.

The young man was heavily built. The girl with him was the most beautiful he had ever seen. She was dark and tall and her figure made more luscious by a shirt and patched workman's blue overall. Suddenly she laughed, turned, put up her hands and shoved the young man into the river. He disappeared in an explosion of water, and as the drops fell she nodded as if counting them. Then she bent with her hands on her knees and watched for him to surface. He came up gasping, shaking his head, hair and weeds plastered over his face.

'You stupid, fatheaded bloody woman!' he cried, amid spitting out water. 'I was proposing to you! I love you!' He shook his fist at her to emphasize the point. 'I want to marry you!' He gouged water out of his eyes.

She stayed bent, hands on knees.

'I love you, too, Hughie, but I've told you we can't marry.'

'Why not, you idiot?'

'Because it's incest.'

'It's nothing of the sort! We are cousins. Cousins marry. Cousins are always marrying.'

'Your sister was my mother,' the girl said.

'Half sister! She was my half sister!'

Hicks was fascinated. He watched them arguing, and as she gave him a hand to get out and braced herself cleverly so he couldn't pull her in. They walked away together, still arguing, he dripping like a melting man.

Hicks remained fascinated. He had an idea for a play about it. He juggled with the idea as he went away. He thought about it all day and all night until it came to him that he was not thinking about a play but the girl.

In his convalescence he pretended he

wanted to start working again and do an article about Rustum Magna and the famous boatbuilder, Tom Rogers. He came with a girl photographer. They spent hours with Tom Rogers and Elizabeth and her young sisters. Hicks asked everything it was possible to know about the Rogers, and the ducked man, Hugh Rawley, whom Elizabeth would not marry. After a week, Hicks made a request.

'You want to marry my daughter?' said Tom Rogers. 'Who the bloody hell are you?'

Tom refused permission, and Tom was right, perhaps, but Bet said he was wrong. When Tom's daughters said he was wrong it did not end there. When he had run out of cotton wool for ear-plugs he agreed.

Bet and Hicks were married at the Saxon church at the top of the village in September, when Elizabeth was 17. Hugh Rawley sent her a great bunch of red roses swearing on a card that they were stained by the bleeding of his heart. She shed many tears, but, for her, Hugh was out of the running, mostly because she feared faulty children from inbreeding.

At the ceremony a journalist from Hicks's paper asked Tom, 'If this is Rustum Magna, where the hell's Rustum Minor?' And Tom said, 'It's the phone box on the Bristol road,' and wept a tear about it.

Christopher Hicks had met fate because he had been shot in the leg by a freedom fighter in Soweto, who had already shot his own father and didn't believe in prison sentences. As soon as the leg was better, he went back to his foreign travels, and by then Bet was installed in their rented London house in Chelsea. Her husband had not told the truth about his real position and Bet was far from pleased when she found out what it was. While he sent back unconfirmed reports from Somalia, she had begun to swell with twins, but he was back on a month's leave for the births.

He was then nursing a flesh wound in the backside inflicted by a member of the Somali Liberation Army who thought he was a Red Cross spy. As Bet was engaged with her new babies during his stay he managed to hide his backside, which was a pity, for had she seen it she would have made him forego any further foreign trips. As it was he did a short investigation into the Red Brigade in Italy and thus was home a good deal, and on one occasion Rosalind was conceived.

He was directed to Chile after that, and there he was at last effectively shot dead by a guerilla outside Valparaiso while driving to interview the guerilla leader, who returned the body to a fellow newsman in the town as an example of the atrocities being committed by the Chilean Army.

Tom Rogers had died just six months before, leaving his cottage and boatyard to Bet and his wherewithal to be divided amongst the other daughters, whose husbands had then taken them far afield. As soon as Bet heard of her husband's death, she thought of the children and the problem of keeping a roof over their heads. She told the agents for their rented furnished house she would leave at once. She had drawn the month's housekeeping the previous weekend and all bills were paid. She piled all their belongings and the children into their Standard Vanguard and drove away to her old home.

When she got there she found the problem was not so much keeping the roof over the children's heads as stopping it falling on them. She set up temporary quarters in the boat-shed with furniture from the cottage and made a nursery in the hand-built body on Tom's old Rover Twelve at the back of the big shed, then set about repairing the cottage.

She was in the act of propping up the end wall with stout timbers when pains began. She went into the office in the shed and called the doctor. Rosalind was born before he arrived, when Bet found that the ideal way of delivery was squatting on the floor.

When the story of her position got round, the village men came and practically rebuilt the cottage in three weeks. She gave all the helpers a slap-up party in the garden edging the river bank, with ham, cheese, home-baked bread and a barrel of beer. Having done that she was broke.

She performed a number of small tasks

in exchange for payment. She wet-nursed the baby at Ham House where Mrs Barnes had dried up, and also for Allie Brett in the village, who had triplets but no husband, although her father was furiously looking for one. She made cakes for the bakery, and did some special sewing jobs for Mrs Barnes, and was on the point of undertaking to repair James Carrier's boat when Hicks's newspaper found her. Until then they had not known where she had gone.

The man from the paper gave her news of compensation, outstanding salary, fees, expenses (estimated, due to unfinished business) and insurance, together with a lump sum from the paper.

At the time of the interview, Bet was rather depressed, for until then she had somehow believed that one day her husband would prove himself another unconfirmed report and walk in the door.

When it came to signing the documents about it, Bet hesitated. At first the man from the paper thought she was stalling for a higher price, because that was the only form of business he had ever come across. But then he wondered about another aspect of her curious behaviour.

'Why didn't you get in touch with us?' he said.

'I didn't want to believe he was dead,' she said, looking directly at him. 'But I'm practical as well as a fool.' So she signed.

She was then well-found financially, but, hating idleness, started a private herb business, her mother's hobby. She found a lot of old books of her mother's describing the cures herbs effected and the improvement to normal life they could achieve. She studied. She planted. As the children grew up the National Health Service began to weaken its hold over Rustum Magna, because Bet's medicinal herb values took a lot of unnecessary business away from them.

She kept the boatyard in first-class order and constantly thought of opening it up again, for so many letters came in wanting Tom Rogers's real wooden boats, after some years of plastic craft. But she didn't get round to finding a craftsman able to take on the work her father had done, largely by himself.

Bet did well with herbs. Almost every man for miles around insisted on herbal treatment for all things from dandruff to athlete's foot and came in person to collect his package, unless his wife insisted on running the errand.

Early on in her cottage industry, Bet gained her witch status. Bill Haynes was in the village tug-of-war team but he had a swollen ankle and didn't know how he'd got it.

'I'm supposed to pull tomorrow, but I can't like this. I can't stand on it. It's murdering me. Hot as blazes it is.'

Bet consulted her mother's book, and said, 'Have you got clean feet?'

'Yes. I've been bathin' it to cool it off.'

'Take your boot and sock off,' she said, looking in the book again. 'Stay sitting down. OK.' She pulled up a stool and sat down facing him. 'Give me your foot.'

'It's there,' he said, giving it. 'It's there. All red.'

'Yes, I can see,' she said. 'Hold still.' She got hold of his ankle between her hands and pressed it hard. 'Does that hurt?'

'Not when you press — no. It's when you let go it will.'

She held it for a couple of minutes, then almost threw it at him and got up. He sat with his mouth open.

'Now what?' he said. 'It's hurtin'.'

'It's rheumatism,' she said. 'You'll have to wait till it goes, Bill. It will.'

He was pleased she had held his ankle. It made him feel better at heart but not in foot. But when he had tea at home he suddenly looked up.

'Christ!' he said. 'It's gone! It's bloody gone!'

His mother was surprised.

'Well, that's good,' she said.

'You know what?' Bill said. 'I reckon she's a charmer!'

'Witch, more like,' said his mother.

So easily is a witch born.

But, perhaps, so are authors. Using her mother's books and notes and her own findings and further notes, she wrote some articles on herbs and their uses and sent them to her husband's old paper. They took them at once. Not only did the articles advise on herbs, and people's weaknesses, with some humour, but they gave a name which linked the author directly to their heroic ex-correspondent. The articles grew in number, and became books on cooking with herbs, curing with herbs, beauty with herbs, decorating with herbs, scents from herbs, herbs in Shakespeare, herbs and the Romans, herbs and Greek beauty, health and herbs, until it seemed the permutations with herbs were as inexhaustible as they were profitable.

2

From their earliest days the twin girls were bright, pretty, full of life and natural impudence and very skilled in the use of intelligence. The youngest girl, Rosalind, was as inward as her sisters were outward. She was beautiful rather than pretty, but very much a loner and a dreamer. Whatever she dreamt about made her happy, for she always looked content, and sometimes gleeful over her seclusion.

At 13 she began to plump and take on the beauty of the Botticelli kind.

When they were 15, the twins showed such promise at school that they were offered the chance to take a year at a New England High School on a pupil exchange. They went with Bet's full approval and secret regret. But she still had Rosalind to keep her company during the girl's off-dream times.

Approaching 15, Rosalind's comely beauty hid other changes in her which did not become apparent until the proceedings were very far on. Bet was astounded.

'You never told me about a boy,' she said.

Rosalind smiled softly and looked very happy. 'No,' she said.

'Which boy was it?'

'I haven't got a boy, Mummy.'

'My dear little Roz, there must have been one, mustn't there?'

'I've been out with one or two. They're not very nice, really. Soppy or dirty. I suppose I'll change.'

'You've changed already, dear. Was it a man, then?'

Roz looked vague. 'No,' she said and shook her head slowly.

Bet left that line of questioning, believing that the facts would come out later. For the present she believed it necessary to look after the girl and make preparations. She had an animal's acceptance of life as it came along and handled her difficulties on that basis. Apparent disasters very often turned into small benefits, she had found. Husbands got shot; children got pregnant. It was not the first time in the world such things had happened.

Bet saw the headmistress. As the summer holidays were to begin not far ahead, they agreed Roz should stay away until the autumn term.

The girl appeared to take little interest in the preparations. If anything, her dreaminess increased, and throughout that time and after she said there was no man or boy.

Bet thought the girl was protecting somebody, but the consistent refusal to name anybody or talk about it made it impossible to imagine Roz getting into the situation in the first place.

The girl had followed her grandmother's footprints, and gave no warning signals.

She and Bet were visiting Rosamund Willis in the orchard of Old Will's Cottage, when the girl began to gasp and put her hands to her belly.

'Good God! It's happening!' cried Bet after inspection.

'I'll fetch hot water!' old Mrs Willis said, turning her wheelchair fast and heading for her kitchen. 'They always fetch hot water,' she told herself as she sped in through the doorway.

Bet joined her to borrow towels and other things. By the time Bet got back, Bobby Miller had dropped into the world while his mother squatted on the grass, naked. Roz registered an expression of puzzlement, and then started to cry. Bobby Miller also started to cry.

Rosamund Willis thought it the most beautiful thing she had ever seen, and wrote a new poem about apples dropping in the orchard. She had lost her husband in the car crash which had crippled her for life and wrote small daily poems for a daily paper about finding happiness in the small everyday things of life. Bobby Miller lasted her quite some time. She became his godmother and stand-in aunt.

Seven days later, Roz ran away with a man of God, in the sect called Yahweh's Callers, and became isolated from all who had known her, as her grandmother had done before, to a higher class of worshipper.

Bet became mother in all senses and after three days of the desertion, she fed the child herself. Even accounting for her reputation as witch and charmer, suckling the infant was altogether too extraordinary.

People said strange things. 'I mean, we have to and cows have to . . . ' — 'But goats don't' — 'Oh, no, so they don't' — 'But goats — I mean, cloven hoofs and all that' — 'And some animals do when they think they should' — 'And of course, she's so clever with herbs, and you can do almost anything with herbs' — 'And there's an American who says you can, anyone, if you want to . . . '

The matter was in discussion in the Rectory when the vicar's wife entertained her friends to tea, while the vicar sat eating cake and finishing the crossword.

'The answer probably is she has two large black nipples and a little one on her tummy for the — you know who.'

The vicar put his cup on the table.

'She hasn't,' he said, and walked out.

The room was silent a while before it began to seethe.

The vicar walked down through the village, and turned off through South Wood and came out by the cottage, boathouse, hard and slipway. The top half of the cottage door was open. He glanced aside at Bobby Miller in his pram standing in the shade of the elm behind the boathouse, then tapped. He heard Bet typing inside.

'May I come in?' he said.

'Of course. I've just made tea. Come in. Sit down.'

'I don't want to interrupt your writing.'

'I wouldn't let you. Cake?'

'I've just had cake. Frozen cake. I almost broke my tooth on the frozen cream. I wish Clara wouldn't do it. Everything goes in the freezer. It's like a frozen rubbish dump in there.'

Bet poured tea.

'You want something, Jim.'

'I want to *know* something, but first I'll explain. For the last couple of years round summer on to September, there have been so-called sightings of fairies or ghosts or pixies or whatever in Bell Wood. It's always women who come and tell me. Miss Wainwright, Mrs Forth. The sensitive creatures.'

'Or slightly hysterical,' Bet suggested.

'Ah, yes,' he said. 'As a result of these — visions, shall we say? — I looked up some of the old papers the previous vicar, Willums, left. There are tons up in the loft. I think he meant to publish some day. Anyhow he has a record of a complaint made over thirty years ago, when he was actually asked to exorcise. In the three years we've been here this faint suggestion has cropped up twice. Miss Wainwright yesterday, in fact.'

'She saw men in the wood,' said Bet.

'No, I'm guessing, but it's always men. She has a personal incubus that follows her around. Never mind. It's old, this legend or haunting or whatever it is. We had an archaeologist here, some years

58

back now. He said there were remains of a stone circle in Bell Wood. He used dowsing and found remains of a wood temple long buried. Ley lines crossing. You know about them?'

'Yes. But I've not heard of a stone circle anywhere that's smack bang on the side of a river.'

'The river wasn't in that bed then. These things alter as time goes on. There was a landslide on Bell Hill about 725 AD, so the man said. Anyhow he reckoned such places were inclined to give visions from time to time.'

'Have you ever seen anything there? You must have known it all your life.'

'Yes. I've seen things. Sometimes I was in the mood to believe in fairies but as I got older I wasn't. I thought it was stars shining in the water and sparkling up on the trunks and under the leaves of trees there. Obviously there's something that gives strange reflections and shadows around that area. For all I know they are ghosts. Why not? I never forget the story:

''A man tapped me on the shoulder.

59

'Do you believe in ghosts?' he said — and vanished' '

Jim laughed, then looked quizzical. 'There is one thing that's puzzling the whole village, Betty.'

'About me?'

'How do you manage to feed that baby?'

'To you, Jim, I'll confess. I don't know. It was like this. Roz fed him and then, as you know, went, leaving just a note asking me to look after him. I tried to feed him bottles. He wouldn't have any of it. I got distressed. He just would not feed at all from a bottle. I asked Dr Richardson to find me a girl. After all, I'd done the same for others when I had too much. He couldn't find one right away. You see, getting just the milk wasn't any good. The baby wouldn't take a bottle. And then, well, I don't know if it was stress, or wishing or what, but suddenly I found I could do it. It seems as much like a miracle as anything that could happen, but it happened, and thank God, it has worked splendidly, as you know.'

'Amazing,' he said.

'It's confirmed everybody's suspicion

that I'm a witch, but I can bear that burden, so long as they don't start imagining Bobby's the devil.'

'I hadn't thought of that,' he said, sharply.

'*They* will,' she said.

When he went he came back in again a minute later.

'You always contrive to make me forget what I've come about,' he said, parking his hat again. 'The christening.'

They discussed the arrangements.

'You'll let me know the godparents, Betty,' he said, watching the feeding child. 'Tell me — ' he frowned, ' — how Miller? Have you found the father?'

She sighed. 'Dear Roz always swore there wasn't one. I never got her to admit, and I never will now, I fear.'

'So you picked it out of a hat?'

'Oh no. I reasoned it out, that if there was no father he is a product of the mills of God.'

He stared, then began to laugh, then he laughed heartily.

'You should be ashamed of yourself!' he said.

'Why? Would it do me any good?'

3

1

In March of the last year, Bobby's headmaster called on Elizabeth Hicks and said he had been concerned for some time about the boy's startling mathematical ability.

'The boy has most remarkable gifts, Mrs Hicks. Confidentially, we just can't catch up with his mathematics. He is quite extraordinary. The most complicated calculations are put to him and he gives the answers straight away. He either does not know how he does it, or he just does not care to explain. Sometimes he will stay silent for a few seconds before he gives the answer to a problem put to him, but it is all quite effortless. And this ability naturally flows over into complicated geometry, quite beyond us at the school.

'For instance, playing cricket, now. The batsman hits a ball up into the air.

Normally a boy runs to catch it his face upturned, watching the ball the whole time before he can catch it. Bobby watches the stroke and appears to calculate the geometrical pattern with the speed of the ball and the opposing speed of the bat and from that he knows the angle the ball will take and the trajectory. All this takes him a split second. He then goes to an exact place, holds out his hands and the ball falls into it. We have carried out tests on this very odd ability. He knows how he does it. He has explained the speeds, the angles, parabolas of flight, but how does he see the data? How does he get the speeds so accurately? *and* the windspeed and direction?' The speaker laughed. 'I don't mind admitting that the staff is floored by it.'

'I have been puzzled by some of the things he can do,' Bet said, 'but it has seemed to me that when he has to think before he does something, he finds it difficult, and often gives up.'

'Ah yes! We have noticed that only too often, I'm afraid. In English, history, French, Latin — all these other subjects

63

leave him, not unable, but untouched. He can be obstinate to the point of stupidity sometimes. He'll have to continue with them, of course, and we shall have to strive with him to have his response.'

'Is he good at cricket?' Bet said.

'No. He is unable to grasp the idea of being part of a team. He bats by taking mighty swipes, but his physical skill does not enable him to take advantage of his ability to calculate speeds and directions of the ball. Often he scores well, and just as often he gets a duck.'

'Is he so obstinate about all subjects but maths?'

'His geography is well above average. In fact I would say his interest in the Earth, its structure and its flora and fauna is considerable.

'The reason I came is that we have all agreed on the staff that his exceptional abilities and selective interest should lead him into the science of astronomy. As it is,' the headmaster sat back in his chair with a faintly baffled expression, 'the only thing he wants to do is work on a farm with animals.'

'I know,' Bet said.

'My wife and I must go to London in the Easter term. I would like to take him for two days, show him the Planetarium. I also have a friend who is a member of the Royal Society who would be very interested to meet Bobby. In fact, with his extraordinary gift, there must be thousands of people who would like to meet him if they knew.'

'I don't want him to be treated as a circus exhibit.'

'Exactly. That sort of exploitation must be guarded against very strictly these days.' He smiled and passed his cup for more tea. 'Was his mother a mathematician, Mrs Hicks?'

'No. Poetry was her strongest point. I can't trace this numbers career at all. I can just about balance the housekeeping. My late husband was a writer, his father a builder, and my father, as you may remember, built boats. So I know of no one who could have left him this gift.'

'Has he always had this gift?'

'Er — yes. I think he has. But it isn't the sort of thing that comes to the fore often with a grandmother. He talks of all sorts of things; nature, imaginative stories he reads, food of course, me, our family, worlds, planets, comets, but figures? No.'

'He doesn't *talk* about them to anyone, Mrs Hicks. He just performs. It's impossible to get him to say how he does it.'

'Headmaster, even I know that he is rather an odd boy in many ways. I don't think I have ever got quite used to some of the — surprising things he can do, and does. But that said, he is a perfectly normal boy. All children have their secret lives — I suppose we all do, come to that,' she laughed, 'and sometimes I think that his comes to the surface a little more often than usual.'

'Yes, Mrs Hicks. You are right there.'

2

The old doctor arranged the pillow behind his head, then sat back in his big wing-chair. He regarded the two men over the tops of his half glasses.

'I don't usually give interviews now, you know. I've retired five years ago, and old men forget. Especially old doctors. We knew so many people. It's quite impossible to identify every bellyache, every cut, bruise, boil and pustule, and that's how we remember so many of our patients, you know.'

'Do you remember Elizabeth Hicks, the eldest daughter of Tom Rogers, boat builder in Rustum Magna?' the fair man said gently.

'Betty! Oh yes. The most beautiful girl I can remember — leave out my dear wife, of course — and she still is a most beautiful woman. Oh yes. I was there — not when, but just after, she was born. Most extraordinary family. They don't so much give birth to their children, they rather drop 'em, like fruit. I've never come across anything like it. Her mother was helping Tom build a boat when she suddenly produced, and I came galloping up half an hour later. Then Betty — I don't know what happened when her first were born — twins, you know — as that was in London — but she did the same as her mother with the third. Dropped the youngest daughter on the boathouse floor and I, as before, galloping up too late.

'And then, damn me if the same thing didn't happen to her daughter in the orchard at old Will's Cottage. You know about that, do you? Ah. Will was an old widower living there. He was very fond of children and gave them buns and sweets, and then one day a little girl was found floating in the river pool just below Bell Wood, and the villagers thought Will had done it, because the child had been strangled first, but not quite killed, so it was murder. The accusations got so bad the villagers went and hanged him from one of the trees in the orchard, and the day after, so upset by the hanging and so forth, the blacksmith confessed devils had told him to do it, and that time the villagers did nothing about it. Odd, isn't human nature?'

The fair man contained his impatience. His older companion was more interested.

'When was this?' he asked.

'Oh, er, 1825, I think it was.'

The fair man managed a brief smile, then pressed on.

'Elizabeth Hicks's husband was a foreign correspondent, was he not? Did you know him?'

'I treated him once. He'd had a leg badly shot up. It was very painful at the time, but Bet cured him more than I did.' He laughed again. 'They went to London then, until he went abroad again and got shot more definitely.

'It was all quite a while back now, but I knew Tom Rogers and his family so well. When I was new here I used to take my day off, fishing if I could. I would go down and fish off Tom's little pier. A big elm shades it from the afternoon sun in summer. We'd both sit on the end there, listening to the insects hum, watching the fish go by our lines and talk about what was wrong with the world. When we grew older we'd sit there and puff our pipes and watch other fish go by and by then we'd decide there wasn't that much wrong with the world because it wasn't meant to be perfect in the first place.'

'May I put a personal question, Dr

Richardson?' the dark man put in, and receiving a hand wave of assent went on, 'Do you believe in God?'

'Oh yes,' the old doctor said pensively. 'But not the sort of God that gets peddled around as some kind of human being. I believe in a god who made all this and everything else, but I've never thought that He believed in me!' He laughed quietly. Then he said, 'Why did you ask me that?'

'Because of what you said about yourself as an angling philosopher,' the dark man said. 'For some reason, I wanted very much to know. I can't tell you why.'

'The grandson, Bobby Miller,' the fair man put in briskly. 'He was born in Will's orchard, and he was the young girl's son?'

'Oh yes. No doubt of that, although gossips in the village never got over the fact that Bet suckled him. It was very unusual but not unknown. Many gossips said Bet was the mother, blaming it on the daughter. Rubbish, of course, but the child was very young, really. Fifteen, or only just. I don't remember exactly, but she was a robust child and recovered very quickly. She ran away — oh, it couldn't have been much more than a week after. That was how Elizabeth took on being mother, but as she said then, she'd always been a good cow. She wet-nursed two or three village children at one time, and she was unusually skilled in the medicinal uses of herbs. I, of course, made professional enquiries about it, mainly from the point of curiosity.'

'But it was very unusual?' the fair man persisted.

'Oh yes, indeed, but one must remember mental attitudes and natural urges can together command exceptional results in bodily performance, in all kinds of ways.'

'We are, as we told you, asking only for reason of research which will be kept entirely secret.'

'So I understand, but then everything's official these days. The more official it is, usually the bigger lie it covers up. However, I don't mind talking of things that can harm no one.'

'The father of the baby was never traced?'

'The boy's father? No. I'm certain of that. In fact, it was a mystery at the time and, to me, still is. She was just not the sort of girl who played around with boys. She was entirely reserved. She dreamed, and you probably know that dedicated dreamers don't like flesh. They are not experimenters. No.' He shook his head. 'I couldn't imagine it. Elizabeth couldn't imagine it and she knew the girl intimately, of course. I remember once she said to me, 'Sometimes I wonder if there *was* a father,' and I must confess I rather liked to ponder on that myself!'

He laughed again. The fair man waited for him to finish. The dark man was getting obviously uncomfortable, as if he thought the questioning was altogether wrong, or unfair in some way.

When they had gone, Dr Richardson telephoned Bet, then went to sleep till tea-time. The maid brought in his tea. He sat looking out of the window and eating muffins.

'Department of *what* did they say?' he asked another muffin.

* ★ ★

Dr Ian Ritchie occupied the small wing of the Vicarage which had been divided from the main house. Millie Olney, farmhand's wife, did his housekeeping. She was a cheerful, perceptive woman, comic, earthy. When Ritchie looked glum or worried she would say, 'What youm needs is a good fat woman,' and offer to give him one.

Her husband, having lost a favourite pigeon one day, got jealous, accused her of deceiving him and implored her to stop it by blacking her eye. She then blacked his, kicked him privately and walked out proclaiming, in that street of many ears, she would go and live at the Vicarage.

The vicar's wife, Clara, hearing of this, took alarm since she had an underhand affection for Ian Ritchie and a small jealousy over what she thought he was up to in his private life, which nobody in Rustum really knew anything about. She felt such alarm by the Olney threat that, meaning to stifle any rude gossip before it began, she decided to make a diplomatic intervention.

But when she went to see Ritchie in the barn so as to be discreet, he was at his most irresistible, eyes shining with inner pleasure at having her there and his half smile of ruefulness at having displeased her made her feel she should almost kiss him better, but she knew damn well what would happen if she got to kissing him again, after last Christmas under the mistletoe when innocence had changed to such tense pleasure that she had begun to wonder if she had been quite so innocent in the first place.

'Of course, just as you would like,' Ritchie said and kissed her hand and held it, and she let it lie lank in his light grasp as if she couldn't make up her mind whether she wanted to let go or not, but was hoping some third person might decide for her.

'You do see,' she said apologetically and took her hand from him. 'I mean, I do hate to . . . But in the Rectory, you know . . .'

'Of course I know, Clara. Of course. I knew at once. That's why I said no, and she went back home. A wee bit relieved, I thought.'

'You let me go on!' she said, with a flash of anger.

'Of course I let you go on. I like to hear your voice, Clara. Sometimes I feel I love — '

'No!' she said and went to the great doorway. 'No. You're just damn naughty, Ian!' And she walked out, tall, long-legged and in rather a hurry as if he might be chasing her.

Ritchie sat on a hay platform and looked up to where the arch of the great doorway met the sky. Two small birds had sped in and wheeled in the vastness of the great roof as if making a survey, then they flew to the remains of last year's nest, stuck to the side of the beam by the door.

'The swallows are back,' he said. ''Tis spring again, and the birds fly in from the great map of the world, coming in to this little place with unerring aim — this is for celebration.' He went into his office and workshop at the end of the barn and came back with a bottle of Scotch and a glass. He sat on the hay platform again and for three hours watched the two birds fly in and out with building materials to repair the old nest.

Bobby Miller came in and joined him, sitting feet up on the hay platform hugging his knees.

'They're early,' he said, watching one bird come back with a beak full of rough grass. 'Three weeks.'

'Well, summer's early,' Ritchie said. 'Here lad, go and fetch some sandwiches for my lunch. Salmon and cress. Catch Annie before she goes off to bed. Get some buns for your wretched self.'

The boy took the money and went slowly towards the great doorway, staring upwards.

'But how do they know?'

'I wish I knew. It's navigation plus. They come five, six, seven thousand miles direct to the little pinpoint stuck on a barn wall. Bloody amazing.'

'I didn't mean that. I mean how do they know down in the middle of Africa that the summer's early here?'

He laughed and ran off. When he came back with the sandwiches Ritchie had worked it out.

'They get the feel off the ocean winds,' he said.

'You know they don't,' Bobby scoffed. 'It's the wrong hemisphere, and they cross the Mediterranean, and it's been bad down there.'

'So how?' said Ritchie, opening the sandwiches. He always encouraged the boy to let his imagination swell out into fantasies. Bobby had a gift for that as well as figures.

'They pass it on,' the boy said. 'That's what they do when they sing first thing in the morning. Telling each other about the weather. Then birds go to France, and birds go on to Morocco, then different sorts of birds fly down the coast, and pass it on to the middle of Africa, and the swallows hear it and say, 'Right! It's warm up there now, so off we go!''

Ritchie shook his head.

'I wouldn't like to think that all that beautiful chorus of birds in the morning is nothing but a chattering of news and weather forecasts. No. You go home and bring me something more spiritual, more magnificent.'

An hour later two men came in at the doors. There was a fair man and a dark man and Ritchie looked at them with his head on one side as he slowly munched a sandwich. The fair man showed him his card.

'Is this your security?' the fair man said, jerking his head at the open doors.

'Traditional,' said Ritchie. 'Kept open all summer. The swallows nest up there, you see?' He pointed.

Both men looked. The dark man stayed looking. The other turned back quickly.

'Swallows? You keep the doors open because of swallows? Is this the sort of security you employ here?'

'Security, security,' Ritchie said, as if singing a dirge. 'What security do I need? This isn't a Government germ warfare establishment. This is Sloppy Joe's Comic Atomic Hook-up Do-it-yourself shop.'

'That's an old nest,' the dark man said. 'They're repairing it. How long has it been there?'

'They've been using that one four years. You see the remains of two old ones further along the beam.'

'That's your office?' the fair man said.

'Office, workshop, lab, lavvy, shower, whisky cellar. All portable metal divisions. The whole lot can be dismantled, removed, and the barn left as original.' He looked at the fair man. 'You're part of the Government service. You would know all about this already.' He took a sip of Scotch. 'That's why you came.'

The fair man looked to the metal walls, puny in the vastness of the barn.

'You are a distinguished man of science, Dr Ritchie,' the fair man said, turning back. 'What happened last night?'

'The universe stopped. A sidereal hiccup. Interesting, but I don't think we should ponder too deeply.'

'Why not?'

'You might drown in your own nightmare. Man has but a very small brain, sir. It doesn't match universal affairs.'

'Do you think it could have anything to do with the lost X24?'

'Snark? It may be a Boojum, but it couldn't do what happened last night. It could, perhaps, like the nail of the shoe of the horse of the soldier of the cavalry whose stumble lost the war. But perhaps, only. And the effect, if there was one, could be only local. You might, by a miracle of balancing one effect against another create a wobble in a small planet if you were very, very unlucky, but that would be the most extreme possibility. Last night the solar system — at least — hesitated. That's quite beyond the wit or accident of man.'

'Well, nothing's happened since,' said the dark man. 'Or has it?'

'I don't think so.'

'Beautiful village,' said the fair man. 'A young friend of yours made quite a mark in London around Easter. The Planetarium, Science Museum. The head-master took him up there.'

'Bobby Miller,' Ian said. 'The preco-cious mathematician. Yes. I came here just after he was born. He's always been very bright. I didn't know he'd caused a riot.'

'Well — so to speak,' said the dark man. He smiled. 'He set the scientists back a little. The headmaster shunted him around. Trying to get him a place at

Cambridge, perhaps.'

'Too early for that,' Ritchie said. 'To channel his mind into what he's best at would leave him half educated.'

'You work here alone, doctor?' the fair man said.

'I am an invention of Sir Hugh Rawley. He had a dream of recreating the lone inventor of old in the hope I might think of something new. If I do I put it on the line to his lab and they kick it around and build it and test it and bugger it up and finally make something commercial of it. I am alone with nature. I please myself. If I want anything I ring HQ and they send it within two hours. I am a king with no subjects; no discernible responsibility. If I get something wrong, they find it and tell me.'

'Does it keep you busy?' the dark man said blankly.

'If I'm not busy with an idea, I get on with my book on the vanishing lairds. The only thing about writing is it tends to get me drunk.' He looked from one to the other of the men. 'What have you come for, exactly? A wee chat?'

'A social survey,' the fair man said. 'We're doing districts at a time. Industry, agriculture, numbers employed . . . '

Ian did not listen. He smelt something fishy about this visit, but did not know why.

'May we look at your office-cum-workshop?' the fair man said.

'Yes,' Ian Ritchie said. 'But it isn't representative of the neighbourhood.'

The fair man looked at him sharply, then turned towards the office as Ritchie got off the hay platform.

4

1

On the afternoon of 14 June some members of the Cabinet met the Prime Minister in Downing Street. The main subject to have been considered was how to admit the loss of the cruising weapon, X24, the Snark. However the main subject for discussion became the halt of the solar system at around 2 a.m. that morning.

Were the two connected? World reports from local expert opinion varied slightly from yes to no, though some expert opinion naturally did not know about such a cruiser as the Snark. So the total of opinions fed into the computer together with the degrees of ignorance presented in each case produced in answer a positive 'Nes'.

The Cabinet discussion then mainly concerned the question; For how long should we say nothing?

The only thing thought worth leaking to the Press was a brief moment when Defence spoke of something 'reaching a state of maximum saturation'. Science replied, 'Rubbish. Saturation *is* a maximum,' to which Defence came back, 'Since when have we been in the business of using words for what they mean?'

★   ★   ★

The same day, at 6.30 p.m. the Carnival Committee met in the long room on the first floor of The Bygone Arms. The room had served for all kinds of committees, brotherhoods, sisterhoods, farmers' societies, unions, weddings and inquests. Its size, massive timbers, great stone fire, giant-size long oak table, all usually gave an impressive air of security, but, somehow, not that day.

'It was *dreadful*,' said Miss Wainwright, fidgety, mousy, alarmed secretary of the committee, the Parish Council and any other corps at which she could bow her head and scribble industriously. 'I thought I was dying. It was the awful awful *silence*. And after, I'm sure I could hear things moving in the house.' She lowered her agitated voice to a whisper. 'Have you ever heard my house was haunted?'

'Not in my forty years,' said chairman Maud Wise, and frowned. 'What was it last night? Have you heard anything? On the wireless? Has anybody heard what happened last night?'

'Nothing happened,' Annie Bettys said. 'I was up, starting a batch. It was the most frightening thing, because *everything stopped happening!*'

'What do you mean exactly?' said Fred Gage. 'I woke up, and thought there had been a bang.'

'I thought that!' said Clara. 'Yes, I thought it was a bang.'

'What did vicar think?' asked Flo Brett.

'He woke up, too,' said Clara. 'But he said he thought his heart had stopped a beat or something.'

'I thought the world stopped going round,' said Flo.

'But wouldn't we all have fallen off?' said Clara.

'Where to?' said Fred Gage. 'There's nowhere to fall. It isn't up or down, out there.'

'I'm not going to think about that,' Clara said, after a moment's thought. 'If I think about space and all that I begin to think I might not be really here at all.'

'My Bert says it's a warning to stop all this sinning. Sodom and Gomorrah, he said. The Lord drowned it in salt.'

'The Lord turned Lot's *wife* into a pillar of salt,' said Clara, kindly. 'Because she looked round when He'd said not to.'

'Well, if my home was being struck down by the Lord or anybody else I'd have bloody looked till me eyes popped,' said Flo Brett. 'Is vicar coming?' She looked round.

'He's sent his apologies,' said Clara. 'He has gone to Kidderminster to bury an old friend.'

'Funny thing to do to an old friend,' said Fred Gage, depressed by the talk up till then. But nobody laughed. 'Well, are we going to have a meeting then, or is it the end of the world or what?'

'What made you say that?' said Miss

Wainwright in sudden anxiety.

'Dr Ritchie said it this afternoon. I was fillin' up his Land Rover. He said, 'Gage, it is the sign from Heaven! We're all for the big chopper in the sky.' That was because I asked him what he thought it was, of course.'

'He was joking!' said Clara.

'Yes, he does joke,' said Miss Wainwright. 'Sometimes I think he likes to frighten people.'

'And sometimes he does frighten people,' said Flo Brett. 'Up there with all his chemicals and electrics, I wouldn't be surprised he wasn't making another Frankenstein up there.'

'And p'r'aps he made that clatter-bang in the night with his secret fireworks,' said Fred Gage. 'But time's getting on. Are we going to have a meeting about the carnival, or are we going on about the end of the world? I want to know. I got a job to finish back at my garage.'

'Yes. Order, please,' said Maud Wise, surfacing. 'Let us get the business over. Miss Wainwright, please read out what was arranged about the band and what has been the result of the letter from the committee.' She banged the table with the resident gavel, missing the block provided. 'Please take your seats.'

* * *

'I need clarification of your report,' said the Minister, tapping the file on his desk. 'Are you suggesting there is some sort of conspiracy protecting the boy?'

The dark man looked quizzical and faintly amused as he allowed the fair man to answer.

'Conspiracy no, Minister. But as you see, Sir Hugh Rawley is related to the boy, and Ritchie is distantly related to Rawley. Both have known the boy since birth and are in the capacity of guardians, because the grandmother is a widow.'

'But you had most difficulty with the aged grandmum?'

'You should see the aged grandmother, Minister,' the dark man said. 'I put her down as mid-thirties when I met her. It turns out I was ten years short, but she is a quiet, beautiful woman. Graceful, charming and gifted. And when she guessed we were trying to pump her she just tied us up in knots. It was a pleasure to watch sheer skill like that.'

'But she is not normal,' said the fair man. 'She is thought to be a witch.'

'You often get that sort of thing in backward villages,' the minister said. 'You know that.'

'Consider this,' the fair man said. 'The boy is her daughter's son. The daughter disappeared just after the birth and the grandmother mothered him in all senses, and she was then 33, and there was a witness at the time of the birth that the child was the daughter's, and Elizabeth Hicks had not been pregnant. It was a wonder at the time, and confirms the witch suspicion.'

The minister thought a moment, then referred to the report again.

'You say the boy is peculiarly gifted at mathematics, and this is and has been a source of great interest to Dr Ritchie.'

'The boy was around all the time Ritchie was working on the Snark computer and it is possible Ritchie used his mathematical powers now and again, though it seems he checked everything on computers later.'

'You are not seriously suggesting that an experienced scientist of Ritchie's qualifications and esteem would use a kid's calculation to start a project like Snark?'

'It is not for me to suggest anything, Minister. My purpose is to find out what I can of the matter and report to you pointing out where, in my opinion, some facts may have been covered up.'

'You seem to be pointing out that the top people in this matter are influenced by children, and thus behave like children even in matters of grave importance.'

'We all behave like children,' said the dark man, watching the fine markings of the minister's mahogany desk. 'It's pretending we don't that causes all the trouble.'

The minister stared at the dark man.

'Now that I like,' he said. 'But I think it worries me more than this report. In view of what has happened last night, I think you had better go down there again, and keep in daily touch — just in case.'

★ ★ ★

The night of the 14–15 June passed without pause. On the 15th people began to wonder if yesterday's tense anxiety had been worth the strain. The night of 15–16 was also uninterrupted, so the 16th day was one of quiet relief. The strange pause had been a passing phenomenon.

Karel Janacek in a letter to *The Times* said he had found, in some archives in Prague, that a similar hesitation had been recorded by a Jacob Vaselsky of Przl in 1435, which he had published, and then had his head cut off for attempting to create unrest.

Rustum Magna cared nothing for the Maniac of Przl, as only two copies of the paper came to that village; one to Ritchie, the other to magistrate Barnes. Conversation in the street was back to the heat and gossip on sins spiritual, sins probable and especially sins of the flesh.

Mrs Forth, who always looked as if she

was playing Ophelia floating in a watery grave, called at Bet Hicks's cottage in the afternoon. On invitation she sat down at the table and leant on it, her long hair hanging in weeds by her white face. She stared at Bet with a dark-eyed, almost haunted, expression of dread.

'Me man's in pain agen,' she said. 'His back is achin' him out of his mind.'

'He ought to see a doctor. I think he's got a bone out.'

'I told him. I said, 'See a doctor,' I said, and the silly sod said rudery I won't bring myself to repeat. Me man is a right bugger for evil words.'

She always referred to her consort as 'her man' because her husband was living with her consort's wife up beyond Bell Wood in a caravan.

'You can have some more oil if you want it. It will ease the pain, May, but it won't do any good. It's gone on too long. Make him see a doctor.'

'That's harder than makin' him see sense. I tell him, I say, 'This is not good to me, neither,' but he won't take no. Got stuck on top of me last night, the silly bugger. Couldn't move. 'Me back's gone!' he bawls. Took me three hours to get out from under, and him bawlin' and yerkin' not to jolt his back. I said to him, I said, 'What if there's another of them Big Bangs and we're stuck like this? Look a fine couple, all stuck together so you haves to have an amblance to get you off'. But he just moaned.'

Bet looked gravely sympathetic, holding back a tendency to burst.

'I'll get the oil,' she said, holding her jaws tightly in control.

'Oh, and your Bobby,' said May Forth, calling after her in the old scullery. 'He was with Maggie Finch yesterday evening. Saw them on the river bank, playin' about and laughing. All open down her front, she was, showin' her tits and all, and I said to meself then, 'He's a bit young for her,' I said. He's only 13, isn't he? She'll spoil him, she will, that Maggie.'

'Here's your oil,' said Bet coming back. 'Now you tell your Fred to get to the doctor, and if he won't I'll not let him have any more of this.'

'I'll tell him.' She went to the door and

looked back. 'She's 15, that Maggie. I thought I'd mention I saw 'em.' She went off through the wood, talking to herself. 'Now what *would* have happened if we'd had to call for help and him stuck there like that? It don't bear thinkin' of, and me nightie all round me neck . . . Oh dear!' She closed her eyes once more at the horror of what didn't happen.

That had made her forget till then why she had come out of the wood on that spot and seen Bobby and Maggie on the bank. She had thought she was being followed through the wood, but each time she looked back, she saw no one. It was a mixture of excitement and fear she had felt at the time, because once she had been followed through a wood by a man who had given her considerable pleasure by attempting a genteel rape which she had prevented by what Fielding called a 'timely compliance'.

But last night there had been nobody there.

She stopped and almost dropped her bottle as she looked up at the trees and remembered Flo Brett had told her she had thought there had been 'somebody in the wood' following her. And scatty Miss Wainwright had sworn she'd been chased in the wood by a man who kept hiding so she hadn't been able to see him.

Then Mrs Forth thought; Was it a ghost? A ghost? Pursued by a ghostly raper! Goodness!

She hugged herself in a strange delight and decided to walk in the woods that night, while Fred was resting his back.

If there was one thing Mrs Forth liked more than guilt it was goosepimples.

2

The vicar called as Bet started to make tea.

'I thought I saw the Forth departing.'

'She was here about her man's back. I think he's slipped a disc and won't do anything about it. Tea?'

'Yes, please. She's halfway to being a great tragic clown, that woman. She's always wanting to confess, but I've had to discourage that. Her confessions are true enough, perhaps, but they involve so many others so infamously it's like a scandal sheet. Not that, in her case, I suspect too much fantasy.'

'Not like Miss Wainwright?'

'She's been on about creatures in the wood again, strange ghosts and incubi peering round tree trunks at her. But we must not make fun. Mrs Brett has also mentioned it to me.'

'Flo? She seems solid enough, but she is privately keen on fortunes, the future, the stars, the tea-leaves. I think sometimes she's wishing for something to make an honest man out of her wretched husband.'

'The daughter's second husband has turned up,' Jim said. 'He's going to take her away with him this time.'

'I wonder Brett hasn't beaten him up again. He drove that man out of the village as he did the first husband. That poor woman can't have had any peace from that bloody father of hers.'

'It can't have been an easy situation finding a father for a girl with triplets. She shouldn't have stayed in that cottage next door to her parents. That really was the mistake, but then free housing isn't easy to come by. I think Flo herself is quite noble. The way she has defended that man through the years — ' He shook his head. 'Quite unbelievable.'

'You didn't come to talk about her or the others. What is the matter?'

'These two investigators. It is supposed to be a social survey they are about, but Ian Ritchie and I are both of the mind that their main interest is your Bobby.'

'I had that idea, too, Jim. But why should they be interested in him? His gift for maths?'

'That *is* quite extraordinary, but I wouldn't have thought it would have drawn a semi-secret government inquiry on his head. Ian thinks there is something very odd about it, but he does incline to exaggeration.'

'Inclines? He is exaggeration. He's told me what he thinks. Hugh has, too. They're both suspicious. So am I, but I just can't believe that we could be right. The men have come here on some inquiry and Bobby is a little phenomenon, but only because of his figures. Otherwise he's perfectly normal.'

For a moment she thought of Bobby and Maggie Finch and thought he was growing up normally, too.

'His skill at figures is no secret, then how else can they be interested in the boy?'

'I don't believe they can be, Jim. But then, what on earth can a boy of 13 have about him that attracts the attention of the Government?'

'The father?'

Bet was startled. 'But we never knew who it was! Roz went seven days after Bobby was born, joined a religious sect, went to the States and, as far as I know, is there now. The last two Christmas cards came from Los Angeles, but I don't know if she's there now.'

'Is that all she sends? Just cards?'

'Yes. That's all. She's not like the twins. They write volumes. Also I visit each every two years, as you know. One year to Vermont and the other to Auckland. But Roz, I just don't know where to find her.'

'Not through the sect?'

'It took a long time to find out which

one it had been, and by then she'd left it, much in the same way, I suppose, as she left me. Without any word of where she might go.' She stared past him to the window. 'It was so strange, the whole business. She knew her body was changing, but up to the very moment she gave birth, I don't believe she thought there could *be* a baby.'

'But she knew about life?'

'Of course. I didn't leave the girls in the dark. It spoilt her idea of life being a rosy dream, so I thought. I was wrong somewhere. I suppose one day I shall know the truth about it, but in the back of my stubborn mind I still believe there was something odd about it.'

'But not about Bobby?'

'Oh, of course not!' She laughed. 'And yet there is this small point. As you know, he has family likenesses, ways, small habits by which you can tell he's one of our long family. But there really aren't any traits which could give any idea of what his father was like. It seems that Roz and all nature conspired to erase the father from the affair.' She looked up suddenly. 'Well, it's not an original plot, but I didn't mean it might be a copy.'

'No, I don't think another archangel was involved, dear,' Jim said, and patted her hand.

★   ★   ★

That evening, just after May had gone and Bet was thinking of Bobby and the boat, the man came. He stood in the garden for a minute or two as if not sure where to go, then he came to the cottage half door, which was open at the top. He was broad, dark-haired, sun-browned and with dark eyes. When Bet saw him at the half door, she thought he had a brooding look before he saw she was there.

'I've come down from Stratford,' he said, 'on an off chance. I started building boats with Sanson up there, just up the Avon from the town. It was took over a few years back for repairs and dozzing up old boats, barges and the like. I don't like the repairs so well. I like to build. I knew about Tom Rogers from when I apprenticed. I would like to buy in.'

Bet looked at him.

'Well, that's straight,' she said. 'Come in. Sit down. What do you mean, buy in?'

'Be a partner. I've got money put by. I would satisfy, I think. I know boats.'

'Accommodation is tricky here,' she said. 'Are you married?'

'Not now. No children. On my own. Digs, p'r'aps, till I can get to look round. I don't want to go back, you see. Nothing to go back for. I left. I didn't want to keep repairing. Patching up. That's all it is. Patching. No skill really. No art. There's a Rogers boat here I could finish. I heard about it back in Stratford.'

'My father died thirty years ago. It's been untouched since.'

'I could finish her. Can I see?'

'Have you looked already?'

'Through the window. Yes.'

'Come and look.'

They went out. She unlocked the front double doors of the boathouse. She had kept everything clean inside, 'like a museum,' Hugh once said. He walked round the unfinished boat on the stocks, looked underneath, climbed up on the staging and investigated the work done so long ago.

'I can finish this,' he said.

'There are no drawings. Father just sketched on bits of paper.'

'I know what he'd do,' the man said. 'I read about him and his ways. Magazines. Boat magazines. You know? Old ones. There's a book, too. I've got that.'

He looked down at her. The brooding look had lightened. She had a sudden odd feeling that he loved that boat, as if he'd known it a long time. Her heart warmed. The odd, dark look in his eyes changed, but not to brighten; he glowered.

'I could finish that for him,' he said, clambering down. 'I could do that, no problem. I know his work. I've done two or three of his boats. Old ones, but I know.'

'This has been there thirty years,' she said. 'The wood's dry. And designs must have changed in so long.'

'No problem. That's proper wood, that. I see there's more of the same stacked over by there. Enough for this craft and more. Design? No problem.'

'Well, you take a look round and let me know,' she said. 'But to start it would be best if I paid you for the job. Then we can see what sort of a job you make of it. If it's right, then we'll discuss starting the whole thing up again in Father's way. There was always a market for specialist work. Perhaps there still is.'

'I'll start now. Get my tools. Just want to measure up, get the lines right. I've got everything. If I make up drawings from what he's done, I can get working soon.'

Through the side window she could see a Mini van parked. She wondered if she had made a mistake agreeing so easily, but it was something she had had in the back of her mind for so long she could not resist the temptation to go ahead as fast as George Heald intended to go, now that the possibility had so suddenly arisen.

He gave her an envelope.

'References,' he said, and went out to the van to get his tools.

She suddenly imagined herself looking ahead into a future and then the memory of the midnight stillness returned to frighten her again.

5

For days the world proceeded on its way, mazed only by the extent of the steadiness of the weather over the sphere. The heat continued across the northern hemisphere; winter drought held in the southern. The odd hesitation of the night of 13–14 June faded from the memory of all but astronomers and nightmares.

But on the night of 21–22 June, at roughly the same time as before, pause came again. The extent of the hesitation was longer than the first by 0.527 of a second.

At 23.49 on the 21st, mother control received a signal from the Snark, but owing to the intelligence-defensive equipment (trans.: bloody-mindedness) built in to the wanderer's brain, control could not lock on, and the Snark was lost again.

It was unfortunate that the Snark should have come into the picture just before the second world-gripping phe-nomenon because once again the two were linked in the official mind and Sir Hugh Rawley was telephoned out of his bed at 3 a.m. on the 22nd.

He went back to bed but, unable to sleep, went riding until sunrise and then he rang Ritchie.

'I must see you. Say an hour,' he said.

He had a shower, dressed and went down to the silent kitchen. He stood for a moment at the door, listening; but the quiet was not the silence of the night. This was the quiet of a thousand tiny sounds in the great house and of the birds outside and the moving air; the sound of life.

He cooked himself some bacon and made a sandwich of it and was eating it as he walked to the main door and saw Henshaw coming down the stairs.

'Is everything all right, sir?' Henshaw said.

'Yes, thanks, Henshaw. I shall be out for the morning.'

'I'll let your secretary know — and her ladyship, of course, sir. But I believe she said she would be out to lunch today.'

'Yes. I leave it to you.' Hugh opened the great door and went out. He held the sandwich in his teeth as he got in the Range Rover and went away down the drive towards the road, munching.

The day was hot at 6.0 a.m. He drove right into the barn. Ian Ritchie was in his office.

'Me watching machines record another hiccup in the affairs of the universe,' Ritchie said, as he came out. 'And there's a message on the typer. The Snark was heard in the mountains of the moon and lost. The damn thing gets more like its original every day. Remember?

They hunted till darkness came on,
    but they found
Not a button or feather or mark
By which they could tell that they
    stood on the ground
Where the Baker had met with the
    Snark.

Hugh dropped into one of the office armchairs.

'I was awake last night when it came,' he said. 'It was like a nightmare. I felt I was dead! I seemed to feel I was bound — wound up in a ball of string. I could see, but not hear, or smell or breathe or feel I was alive. I was tied up stiff by something so enormous my head was stunned by the sheer size of the calamity. It was Bobby's bloody giant's boot heel and the fire had sucked all the oxygen up and left everything suddenly dead, petrified as it stood. When it ended I couldn't come alive again for a few more seconds in case I was struck dead again. Let's get some coffee.' He got up.

'I've made tea,' Ritchie said. 'With a little whisky in it no harm can befall you. I'll pour, and talk. Two men called again yesterday. Talked more about Bobby again. I kept getting the feeling it's him they're after.'

'Why? Because he's clever? I had a dream about Bobby and his giant,' Hugh said. 'I asked the giant why he was burning up the universe, and he said, 'Well, I'm God, aren't I?' Sometimes I dream pantomimes like that. But why would they want Bobby? Have they seen him?'

'Well, no. He's at school in the week and governments don't work at weekends. They seem to be interested after his trip to London with his headmaster. He does make a mark, Hugh — '

'No milk and no Scotch,' Hugh interrupted.

' — when he gets on figures and stars and natural forces. Where the hell does he get it all from?'

'It might be a throwback to further than we can see. It is a remarkable gift, but why a couple of government snoops? You must be wrong, Ian. A social survey must be a bore and they've just cottoned on to somebody brighter than the rest.'

'You're probably right,' Ritchie said. He drank a small dram and then sat down to drink tea. 'It is unfortunate our vehicle sends back a signal just before the whole works stops.'

Hugh sat up.

'Couldn't be a warning signal, could it?'

The men stared at each other.

'Now there's a thought,' said Ritchie.

'Throw the phone across,' said Hugh.

The minister was available to speak, but Hugh did the speaking before he did any listening, but once he did listen, he looked a little easier.

'They're off us,' he said, putting the phone down. 'Let me get at that tea.'

'Do you mean they've given up the whipping boy?' Ritchie said, hopefully.

'No. But they're keeping us in reserve, just in case they can blame *something* on Snark,' Hugh said. 'But there is confidential information buzzing about that Jodrell Bank, and that place in California, and that one in the Andes — all the usual watchpoints are reporting small but significant changes in the universe, or so they think. It seems that some stars and pulsars and other drifting rubbish have ceased to give off radio signals and these genii say it's a sign the stars have burst or otherwise disappeared. It's the fringe ones. They think these gaps in the night-time are reactions to disappearing worlds.'

'And what if this process gets a bit nearer?' said Ritchie, and poured himself a little Scotch.

'Well!' Hugh laughed. 'There's nothing we could do about that, Ian.'

'And they couldn't blame us,' said Ritchie. 'So at least there's some comfort in calamity. It's nice to have a quiet shiver, but what you think is going to happen could be so violent that when the disaster strikes you often don't realize what it is.'

'Lawson told me it might be the beginning of another Big Bang, in which case this whole lot will dissolve in flame and in a few million years another universe will form out of the gases, as before. He's always had a fix on everything being a cycle. Same thing happening over and over again.'

'Yes, but not exactly the same, Hugh. That's the point. Nothing ever is exactly the same. But seeing as how he's the chief of your space research and general factotum of the Saturn rings, shouldn't he know what's going on? He's got the data and all the computers God ever made. Do they give no answers to this apparent fringe failure?'

'It's a big universe, Ian. And who was that little Chinese with an abacus who got the answer quicker than that computer. He got the answer while the computer man was putting the question, and he was still quicker than the machine in time taken to answer. It often happens that by going right back to the start one could get a different solution. A lot of our troubles stem from this determination to go on trying to develop from something that was already supposed to be the answer.'

Ian stared at him and put his feet on the desk.

'What *are* we talking about, Hugh? Is the world going to end on Tuesday? If so, amen. But I am sad to know that the little joys that every living creatures knows from little time to little time will be dead forever. That is the only tragedy.'

Hugh stared for a long time. 'My God, you might be right,' he said.

Ritchie got up.

'We'll be all right, Hugh. Bet's finishing the Ark down there. Ark Mark II. Have you ever wondered how Noah did it? The ark was the size of a Mediterranean cruise liner.'

'He had divine assistance and no inspectors to poke around and bugger up production. Lucky old Noah.'

'Going?' said Ritchie. 'Well, see you in Auchtermuchty.'

Hugh turned back. 'You're not on leave?'

'Oh no. I wouldn't leave you to be drowned by the scruff like a Government rat. No, I'll stand by while they decide if poor old Snark is blowing up all the pulsars. Depend on me.'

6

'The question is,' the Prime Minister said, 'how are we to treat this information? It's patently obvious it can't be kept quiet. It isn't as if it's some international development that could be dangerous.'

'It could be the end of the world if it develops unfavourably,' the Home Secretary said. 'But I think it would be unwise to suggest it seriously. The suicides don't bear thinking of. Not just here, but everywhere. And after all that it might not happen. Disaster is so far only conjecture. Radio signals have stopped. Does that really mean the stars have disappeared? After all, our scientific equipment is never faultless. Take the present lamentable situation with this Snark, which has taken upon itself the decision to do what it likes. When it was given a human system of decision nobody thought about built-in bloody-mindedness. In my view the present findings of scientific ironmongery might be in some question.'

'That is a sound argument, so far as our equipment is concerned,' said the Prime Minister, 'but the solar system has twice come to a halt, and that's nothing to do with our detection systems. We are in touch with all foreign governments over this, but as yet we have found it difficult to make any decision as to how best to treat the matter.'

'Leave it to the editors,' Science said. 'They keep an even balance so long as they have advertisers, but of course, you can't have the same confidence in the BBC. They'll do anything to get ahead in the ratings.'

Lord Westbrook, Leader of the Upper House, spoke for the first time in six weeks.

'You all assume that once the public has had the wisdom to elect you to office it then relapses into a state of agitated buffoonery or placid inertia, in which states it is impossible for them to remain alive without your care and attention. On the contrary, these people are as fit as you to decide what is best for themselves in

114

their own conditions. Only a very small part cut their throats in the face of the fearful. At present the people are as aware as you that something very important indeed is happening to the world on which we live. Calm yourselves first, consider every possibility and then tell the people how much you know and let them consider *their* possibilities. Tell them as early as possible. Tell them as things happen. Talk to them. Don't stay up here stuffing everything into the safe. Talk to them as you find out what's happening, tell them. After all, if the old ball is going to burst, it's not for you to keep it to yourself just because you have control of the means of detecting astronomic oscillations. Tell them. Share your fears with them. It'll make you feel easier, and even if it's the end of all things, you'll have made a few friends at the very end, and that would be a belated achievement, but still worth having.' The sixteenth earl gathered up his silver pencil and the day's crossword puzzle and left, humming *Oh God our Help in Ages Past*.

Throughout the world on the day of

the 22nd June there was fear, uneasiness, and in some places panic. Radios in millions were kept turned on in case somebody, somewhere, had discovered what was happening to the world, and could answer the only question that mattered: Was the world going to end?

What appeared to be almost a certain sanity affected governments who, knowing they would find no answer, employed quiet, restrained, careful pundits to talk and say how many things were improbable, and take lessons from nature about caterpillars changing into butterflies and moths and the vagaries of bowel action and what causes sudden shivers. Some had to be constantly monitored in case the quiet, measured, comforting tones began to edge into incipient screams. Nor was it any better when a past Astronomer Royal took the television channels to give a soothing talk as if addressing a highly intelligent and well ordered audience, but ended up with a quiet smile and said, 'The truth is the whole bloody lot is going to burst and as I'm eighty-eight, amen.' He was cut, laughing quietly.

Had there been time, a knighthood would have been bestowed on the announcer who cut in swiftly to say, 'Sadly, Sir Rufften Bass has been taken ill and carried off to hospital by the two nurses who were here with him, just in case of a nervous breakdown.'

Insomnia was rife on that night but nothing abnormal happened. The weather remained unusually stable world-wide, but the man in any street anywhere did not know that unless told. The alarm of the 22nd calmed on the 23rd and had almost faded from consciousness on the 24th.

It was not until 24th June that recording machines brought to expert notice that the full moon due on the 21–22nd, had appeared on time, but had done it again on the 22–23rd and again on the night of 23–24th.

And on the 24th June at midday at Greenwich it was seen that GMT had gone 3.7248 seconds ahead of the sun in azimuth or the sun itself was late.

7

1

The persistent moon disturbed Rustum Magna. Its fullness on the 21st June was as expected, and one or two people whispered, as expected, that somebody or the other was always touched by lunar magnificence. On the 22nd, there was a feeling of something being wrong, but nothing definite until the morning, when farmers and others, who noticed such things, reckoned a second full moon had followed the first. On the day following whispers about mental imbalance here and there was intensified, though the very fact of the intensification proved the whisperers as affected as the lunatics.

The rising of the moon at the same time on the third night spread like unwelcome news. People declared they 'felt funny'. Dogs, noted for howling only at full moon, had howled three nights running; conclusive proof of the super-natural taking effect in Rustum.

★   ★   ★

Ian Ritchie remarked: 'It's a nerve-tearer. The animal is provided with alarm mechanisms which respond to visible and audible threat and create adrenalin. The body and spirit braces to the approach of violence by these warning systems.

'But here there is no violence; no visible threat, no warning sound. There is no sound. The system halts; the moon persists. Everything is wrong, but there is no sound, nothing that can be felt. Our alarm systems are boggled. We know things are going wrong, but have no means of knowing why. We go to machines, computers, skywatchers, spa-cial ironmongery, but when they give an answer we feel it can't be right. We are like the pilot flying in pitch-black, whose only guide is his instrument panel, but such is the quiet unreality of his state he begins to doubt the luminous faces and the sweat getting into his eyes distorts the

119

readings until they suit his belief in himself.

'The world is pausing? The moon has lost its rhythm? Oh, no. My reading must be wrong. Everything is all right.

'There is no nervous provision to accept immense change in a magic silence.'

★   ★   ★

It was later than she thought when Miss Wainwright took the short cut through Bell Wood that evening of the third moon. The dusk was growing. She hurried, then began to go quite fast, almost running. She felt there was someone behind her. As she hurried on she became convinced someone was there. When panic almost choked her she halted, as if she feared her legs would collapse if she went on. Her heart beat hard in her throat and beat drums in her ears. She turned suddenly to look into the gathering dusk and saw the boy in amongst the trees, his face peering over the top of a thin bush. She let her breath go in a tearing wind.

'Bobby! You horrid little boy! You wretch! Go away! Go home! You should be in bed long since.'

He backed away into the dusk. She went on, hurrying still. When she came out into the meadow she looked back, but saw no one in the shadows. She hurried on across the grass like a rabbit scurrying to safety.

But her safety was troubled by the moon. She went in and the house was dark. It was a big house on the street; once a doctor's house, then a vet's, and the front room had been used every Wednesday by the bank, back in the days when service came out to the customer. Then Miss Wainwright had thought of buying it and taking in guests, but she prized her privacy and lived alone.

Until the night of the third moon.

She closed the door always before she turned on the light. When she reached out to turn the switch, she heard someone moving. Once more her heart stopped, then climbed into her throat. Someone had got into the house! A burglar! A rapist! *Squatters*!

She scurried about the house, switching on lights, opening doors, calling, whispering, panicking, scurrying, and no matter where she went and looked in the emptiness, she could hear intruders whispering, moving about, floating in the air above the stairs . . .

She ran down to the stairs, hands to her ears, trying not to scream in case somebody heard in the street. Nobody was there. It was moon people. Moon fairies. Old ghosts roused by the moon. The rustling was the banker counting notes.

She turned out the lights as she came, making shadows to chase her down the stairs. She turned out the last light, almost leant against the front door as she unlocked it, then pulled it open.

There was a commotion somewhere in the street. Perhaps it had been echoes that had haunted. Scared anew, she stepped out. There were people in the street, looking towards Rose Lane. She saw Mrs Olney coming back from there.

'What's the matter?' Miss Wainwright said, tensely.

'Flo Brett's nearly killed him. Her husband. What she's protected and stood up for all these years. Him. Turned on him. Beat him near to pieces with a pick handle. Terrible it was.'

'Good heavens! But why? What happened?'

'There was a row about the daughter. Out in the lane. Seems her husband wants to come back and Brett said he'd kick him out again. Well, then it all came out. Allie just blew up and said he was the father of her three boys. After all this time! What a horrible old humbug he is. Pretending to look for the father all those years!'

'His own daughter!' Miss Wainwright shivered and seemed to shrink. 'Oh my dear lord!' She put a hand to her mouth, turned, went back in and shut the door. She stood in the darkness, covering her eyes and suffering.

After a while she heard the ghosts moving in the house again. She held a hand across her mouth and stared at the stairs. The only light was the moon coming through windows and open doors.

'Gladys!' she whispered, taking her hand away suddenly. 'Gladys! I know it's you! Leave me, for Christ's own sake, Gladys! I've suffered enough, God knows.' Her voice died away. She listened. All was quiet.

She wanted to scream, but dared not.

* * *

'She said they were telling her to go on, beat him, beat him till he died,' Audie Drift said in a half whisper.

'But nobody was there but them,' said Mrs Olney.

'Nobody in the cottage. Nobody in the lane. Nobody was there. I saw!'

* * *

Jeff Wise walked the dog into Bell Wood. The heat was heavy on him; depression was worse. He kept seeing the drunken Brett leaning against the inn door, refusing to go, being told to behave. Then, 'Don' you tell me bloody how to behave, you baker's prick!' Jeff had shoved him out then, but Maud was watching and told Jeff to cool it.

In fact, Jeff had realized, the offensive remark had only fuelled Maud's smouldering resentment.

Then, ordered away from the inn, Brett had gone home and been beaten senseless. He had gone away in an ambulance.

'Things are out of hand, boy,' he told the dog. 'People aren't being what they are. Changing. Different people. What's happening?'

He sat on a rock by the shrunken river watching the moon in the water, shimmering. Fancy that bastard pretending to look for the absent father and sitting on his own foul secret, watching the suffering of his daughter as if she didn't matter any more than a bucket he could kick around the yard. And chasing away the husbands when she got them. It must have been a grotesque sort of jealousy. Ugh!

It was too depressing. He called the dog, but that animal was lying on the moss nearby, laughing with his tongue hanging like a banner. He put it back, closed his jaws and yawned noisily as he got up, then went to Jeff wagging his tail like a big feather in the silver light. Jeff stood up and patted the dog's head for a moment as he tried to shake off the odd little feeling of horror and anger over Allie Brett.

'Come on,' he said, and spat in amongst the trees.

When he got back, Maud was in bed, trying to sleep. He undressed quietly. She was lying with only the sheet over her. He stopped in the act of unfastening his trousers waist when she spoke very quietly.

'Baker's prick,' she said. 'That's what he said. Does *everybody* know? *Everybody*, Jeff? How could you make them all laugh at me like this? Why didn't you go away — some woman away so nobody here would know?' She was silent for a minute or more while he said nothing, but just stood. 'I shall go mad if this heat goes on,' she said.

He sat down on a chair half undressed and looked at her lying so quiet on the bed. He could not think of anything to say to her that would not hurt, so he said nothing. She turned on the bed and looked at him, either to see if in that silence he was still there, or just what he looked like. He was just fanning himself with a slipper.

★　★　★

In the big house Mr Barnes stopped and turned as footsteps were heard running in the hall. They started to go up the stairs, and then there was a sign of hysterical sobbing.

'My God! what's happened!' Mr Barnes rushed out into the hall and looked up the broad stairs. He saw his daughter near the top, crying very passionately. 'Max! What's the matter, darling? Max!' He hurried upstairs calling out and reached the top just as the door of her room slammed shut. 'Joan! You'd better talk to her. She's locked herself in!'

Joan was then in the hall staring up, and so was Ralph.

'Its all right, Dad! Girls do that!' Ralph shouted. 'You know they're all potty at that age!'

'All right, dear!' Joan said in a hiss, and then began to go up the stairs. She hated a row unless she started it, because then he walked away; but when *he* started it, and over Maxine, it was very difficult to smooth things over. In fact, as she saw his face at the stairhead her inside quailed, and she knew it would be a most unrestful night and there would be no peace in the universe.

Even with her mother calling through the door, Maxine went on crying because she could not think of what to do. Her passion, Bruno Witt, had wanted her to copulate in the back of his father's car, and she had refused haughtily and got out but after a while she began to wish she had, so as not to look a fool and a baby and a prude and so he wouldn't laugh at her when he saw her again, but actually she didn't want to because of the atomic blasts there would be at home if anybody found out, and at heart she didn't want to, so she yelled because she was mixed up.

'Darling,' Joan called through the panels, 'nothing's happened to you, has it?'

And in a blaze of light George Barnes realized that if it had, she certainly wouldn't have given it all this publicity, so he left his wife at the door and went down to have a Scotch.

It was when she had cried herself into a state of hiccuping reason that she remembered why she had run from the wood and the car and everything.

It had started by walking away from Bruno, and then she had seen boys in amongst the trees. They hadn't chased her or anything, but she thought they had seen, and that made her shame much worse.

It was because she had seen them that she had run all the way back, but, when she began to think calmly, she did not know why she had run at all.

* * *

'You've been swotting there since teatime, Bobby, now give in. You can't cram it all into your head the night before an exam. You know that. Last-minute cramming doesn't work. Now have some lemonade and cake and go to bed.'

'It's history, Liz,' Bobby said. 'I'm just terrible at history. And geography,' he added, thoughtfully. 'And French and . . . ' He closed his books, got up and kissed her. 'I'm really not much good at anything, Liz. I shall fail, p'r'aps. Oh well . . . '

2

Hugh gazed at the big television screen and the picture of stars and the powder trails of other stars making the moon stand out in relief like a ball suspended in space.

'You see it?' Ian said. 'There's the edge of a big circle right round overhead. A shadow, but it forms a circle. Very faint, but I think it's a disc. The stars at the edge shine brighter where the shadow ends, it seems to me.'

Hugh stared hard.

'What is it?'

'I don't know. It seemed a bit more marked as darkness folded over, and then got very faint. Like it is now.'

'Not interference from somewhere?'

'It's regular. Trace the shape.' He followed the faint edge of the shadow around in the background of stars with his finger. 'See? It's quite perfect. A disc. That's not interference.'

Ian sat on his desk. The screen was the only light in the great barn. Even the moonlight through the doors was faint and colourless by comparison.

'Do you remember the early days when we were working on the anti-radar stuff for Snark?' Ian said. 'At first we got shadows.'

'But there was always a shimmer with them. There's none here. Look! It's shrinking!'

The disc got a little more distinct as it shrank. It was like something going away upwards very fast. Suddenly it shrank to a dot, then vanished. The men watched intently for a while, then relaxed.

'Well?' Hugh asked.

'Don't ask me,' said Ian. He switched on a light. 'Pour yourself a dram and one for me,' he said, lifting the phone. 'I'm going to ring round the eyes of the world.

131

Something might have been tracked.'

'You think it was some *thing*? I think it more likely a summer freak interference.'

'It was too regular,' Ian persisted, punching the buttons.

★   ★   ★

Bet slept uneasily on top of her bed. Her silk nightgown shimmered in the moonlight through the open windows. It had shone on her for more than an hour, as if the moon had finally come to a standstill in the clear sky. It was quiet outside, but not the quiet of the universal silence. That supernatural stillness created its own silence, a hush of breath held still in the awful wait to eternity, straining for the rustling of life returning.

All the doors were open in the house so that if any air stirred in the heat of the night it could travel a cooling way through the rooms.

The boy came out of his room into the corridor, naked, like a ghost moving across the moonbeams from the open doors. He moved slowly, like a sleep-walker, his cheeks glistening with the silver streaks of silent tears. He saw her lying on the bed asleep and went in and quietly, softly, got on the bed beside her. She did not wake, he was so gentle. He put his face against her breast and she was awakened by the soft sobbing of his head against her. She put out her arms and drew him tightly to her.

'Bobby — darling — whatever's the matter?'

His quiet sobbing went on, as if he could not stop it.

'Bobby — tell me. What's happened?' she whispered as if frightened to shock him in case he was still somehow asleep.

'Don't let them take me! I won't want to go back!' His voice was so quiet, so terrified, she could hardly hear what he said. He put his arms round her and clung desperately, hiding his face between her breasts.

She held him firmly and began to stroke his head.

'There's no one who wants to take you, darling. There's no one here but me. You dreamt it. It was a dream. Bobby, darling, it was a dream.'

'No.' He would not look up at her. 'I saw them. They were here — today. I know. I tried not to see them, but I had to. I tried not to remember them, but they kept on and on! I love you, Liz. I love you! I want you! I don't want to go back! I love you!' He pressed against her in a panic as if trying to sink into her body and be safe from his torment.

'I love you, Bobby darling. I won't let you go. You know I won't if you don't want to go.'

She went on talking softly, assuring him. He still pressed against her as if to a last refuge. She went on gently stroking his head, and then gradually he began to loosen his body, as if the terror began to drain away.

He slept while she tried to work out how he had got into such a state. For some reason, she felt he had told the truth in that he did not believe a dream had frightened him but that he had seen something during the day. But 'go back'? Where would he go back to? What place was he frightened of? And he had been frightened. His body against her had been cold, as if terror had frozen his blood. What could have frightened him so much? Where had *they* threatened to take him? And he had said '*go back.*' Back to where? Not school. He liked school for the boys and masters if not for the work. Go back *where*? He had lived in Rustum all his life. There was no other home he had been left at. On holidays she had taken him herself and she could never remember seeing him horrified, or hating a place so that it could become a nightmare to him. What *place*? Who were *they*? For how could he have seen them that day, been terrified and not have said anything to her?

The questions went round and round in her head, and there was no answer that could stop them. He was sleeping quietly against her then, his body warm again. She began to doze, waking now and again with the feeling that, after all, someone was there watching in the heat, and she held him firmly as if to guard him even against the demons of the night. But still on the threshold of sleep she wondered where he could go back to, when he had lived in no other place but this.

★　★　★

'It's earthy, this place,' he said. 'That woman nearly killed her old man. That was a pick handle. Is there a lot of incest about?'

Annie laughed quietly. 'I should have thought you would know more about that than me. You are the social surveyor. Isn't that what you said?'

'You don't believe me, do you?'

She watched the ceiling and the moon pattern from the dressing-table mirror shining up in the corner of the room, and then she looked at him lying beside her.

'I look at you as my cuddly alphabet man who pleases me, so you must be a gentleman somewhere underneath all that Government wrapping.'

'What is an alphabet man?'

'KGB, CIA, MI6, CID — any of those.'

'If I was any of those I wouldn't give you away.'

'If you did I would . . . ' She whispered in his ear.

'That's Rabelaisian,' he said. 'Phew! It's hot. I wonder when it'll rain again.'

'Not until you see a cloud again. Do you know how long it is since we saw one?'

'That puts a cold finger at the back of my neck. Let's talk about you.'

'Let's go to sleep,' she said.

★   ★   ★

'I've made tea,' the vicar said. 'It's too hot to sleep. A cup? Yes?'

She sat up to take her tea. 'Jim, what do you really think is happening?'

He stirred his tea. 'I begin to think this is a true case of God only knows. It makes one think of the mightiness of the universe and I feel myself shrinking so fast I get too small to think. Then it's easy. You just crouch down and hope you won't be trodden on.'

'That's not spiritual in outlook.'

'I doubt whether any real consideration of apocalypse can be entirely spiritual.

137

There are considerations of personal loss which includes the loss in all others around you that brings you into the realm of intense feeling of loss, so heavy that true belief is difficult to maintain. What is happening? It's a hell of a question, Clara. The world stops turning, the sun halts, and in the edges of the universe other worlds begin to disappear, to be silenced after years of signalling their existence, as if the fringe of the vast space is charring at its edges, like the armies of red lines that encroach upon a sheet of smouldering paper.' He tasted his tea. 'What tea is this? It tastes like specially selected muck spreadings.'

The universe was receding. Reality came back with the teapot.

★   ★   ★

The fair man sat at the writing-table in the hotel room. He stared out over the moonlit countryside, his hand resting on the papers over which he had spent so long that night. The birth certificate, the copy from the Parish Register, the records from the Air Ministry, his newspaper's record of the travels of Christopher Hicks; a précis of his articles and reports Hicks had submitted; the network of the designers and test establishments; the manufacturers of the separate parts and the certificates of inspection of the prototype, the dates of the test flights, with records of performance, and the report of the final firing of the Snark. Despite an unlikely appearance, he felt that one thin thread existed between some part of the Snark development and the mystery of Rustum Magna; and the receipt that day of a CIA report from San Francisco had fired his suspicion anew.

He stared out over the silver stillness; the black, silent trees like sentries on the rolling vista of fields, the black lines of marking hedges; the ladder lines of wood rail fences and the black mounds of the distant hills. In every field of the chequer-board of night, he saw a part of the jigsaw he was trying to solve. The drifting on to the scene of headlights, passing in and out of the black shrouds of trees distracted his thoughts. He watched the car come nearer along the winding country road, then turn, suddenly and too fast, into the courtyard of the hotel. The fair man got up and watched the man below leave the car and mount the hotel steps. He looked at his watch, checking the home-coming at a quarter to four. He waited until he heard the door of the next room shut, then went out of the room and knocked on the next door in the passage. He went in. The dark man sat on the bed, taking off his shoes.

'Where the hell have you been?' the fair man said.

'I have been learning how to put a French loaf in the oven,' the dark man said, slinging a shoe across the room.

'I told you not to risk being friendly.'

The dark man sat back on the bed and undid his tie.

'The department have often decided to have me by the balls, but they remain my personal property. And if the joy of my professional life is to continue being paired off with you, then I am fully justified in applying for relief of any sort

that will give me a little pleasure.'
The fair man left.

★ ★ ★

The following day, the 25 June, a certain relief spread in official circles when it was reported that the moon was on the move again, but instead of pausing to catch up, it was making headway to meet the scheduled time on 25 June, thus leaving a halt of two days which it was refusing to catch up. For the thousands of watchers of the universe, the monitors of the sounds of evidence in space, the ministers, the editors and the millions of the fearful, the Day of the Tranquilizer had truly come.

8

1

Rustum Magna was badly shaken. The rest of the world was badly shaken, but Rustum Magna did not give a sod what the rest of the world thought or felt or shook about. In the face of danger from without, Rustum Magna's idea of preservation was to erect the barricades. In that sense, Rustum Magna was only one of millions of tiny worlds on this small planet at that time.

The Parish Council met, as usual, on the last Monday in the month and the elected representatives of the parish sat, and, for once, did not debate the war over the Urselden footpath, and its recurrent right of way problem; nor indeed who was to pay for erecting the bus-shelter at Gurt Corner.

The pipe smoking that evening was slow and pensive. The vicar, as chairman, felt like proposing an end to the proceedings, which weren't proceeding. At last something larger than Rustum Magna's existence had taken the minds of the councillors away from the parish.

Councillor Barnes said, 'Of course, it must be discussed, but on what base? If the universe is, in fact, starting to crack up, there's nothing that can be done about it. We are a part of the universe. But the universe is bigger than human imagination can grasp, and time in the universe can't be seen by us to move at all. So if the universe has started to burn, as somebody said, surely it'll take longer than we can live to reach us?'

'Comforting, comforting,' said Gage, wondering if he would ever be called to pay up his overdraft on the garage. 'But we're getting the shock waves now. How long have they taken to get here? If the answer's a million years, OK. If it's a million seconds, that's worrisome.'

Miss Wainwright kept fidgeting. She took the minutes, but this night there were no minutes to take. Parish work seemed to have come to a sudden standstill, which made disaster more imminent, she felt. The idea of unknown cataclysm had haunted her for days, growing stronger each time she heard somebody talk about the mystery of the world's heart stumbling. But it was consuming guilt which a sense of disaster brought, each day making her more and more frightened to face her maker and say, 'My sister! I wronged her — long ago — I . . . ' But there she stopped. She just could not get her mind to go any further. The secret shame of years was to be brought out in the highest court of them all, and she would stand while they pulled out her entrails, steaming with guilt . . .

Miss Wainwright's imaginings had always tried to create flesh, which was why she had always been frightened of the stuff.

'I think we might close the book, Miss Wainwright,' the vicar said. 'It's proposed we adjourn to the bar and that needs no seconder, nor does it need recording.'

'Oh! — yes — yes — of course!' She felt they were all looking at her, and that somehow she was naked and ashamed.

★　★　★

Two hundred miles away, on the mind's doorstep of Rustum, the head of government and his ministers tried to discuss human life as a savable commodity, as if it actually existed like a block of stone.

'We have at last agreed,' the Prime Minister said, 'that all governments shall pool information received at observatories, radio tracking stations, defence watches, satellite stations — in fact every point on the globe which has an eye in the sky is now reporting in constantly to a central receiving point and forwarded to every government.'

'Unity for the first time ever,' said the Foreign Secretary, ironically.

'And the last time ever,' said Science, even more ironically.

'The computer assumption from all information obtained so far gives a picture that can only be described as the universe being on fire at its outer limits and that the flames are coming towards the centre — wherever that may be,' the PM said.

'Is this consumption moving fast, Prime Minister?'

'Yes.'

'In terms of speeds as we could measure it?'

'It is not possible to measure the rate yet, but it seems to be equivalent to that of an explosion.'

'An explosion from the outside?'

'It isn't believed that it's starting on the outside. Sad to say, we may not be the centre of the universe except to ourselves.' The PM looked sad.

'Can anything be done?'

'Can you stop God?'

'If you mean, it's up to the Churches, since they've become political, where's the benefit? And there isn't any comfort to be given, is there? When it comes we shall all get it at once. There's no building of shelters or digging dugouts. Everything goes. Ground and all. It's going to be difficult to believe it can happen, and by the time we're convinced we'll be dead.'

'The question all governments are faced with is; should all this material become known? It would start panics and create vast shambles — and then, the end might not come. Not everybody's got the balance necessary to face this.'

'It'll be violent on a scale never imagined.'

'It will be violent, but you may not know it. If fire or intense heat reaches the Earth, the oxygen will go into it, that will leave death before there is any feeling of it.'

'In the circumstances, I suppose that might be called an optimistic view.'

'It seems to me that the only thing it is possible to do is to devise some way of making things more bearable.'

'The only way to do that, surely, is not to let 'em know.'

'That is a general view among governments,' the Prime Minister said, sadly. 'But if anyone can advise *something* . . . '

'Surely this is a case of God disposing,' said the Home Secretary. 'I think it is really up to the Churches.'

'If they know,' said Science. 'Have the bishops passed the word on down? They might argue against that on the grounds that worshippers are permanently prepared to meet their Maker.'

The bishop in whose see the rector of Rustum cared for his flock called a meeting of his senior clergy and told them what the scientists had told Government and what Government had told the bishops.

Jim arrived back in Rustum thoughtful, and Clara asked what the bishop had wanted of her husband.

'It would seem,' said Jim, 'that the top heads of the world operation believe the universe has begun to burn up and that means the end of this world and all its poor creatures.'

She watched him for a while, then touched his hand, then clasped it.

'It isn't really a surprise, is it?' she said.

'No. And there is truly nothing one can do. Is there?'

'Surely the only thing is to go on living normally. If it will come, there's an end. But to feel dead now isn't what I would like to do. Nor am I going to pray all day. There's not much difference between that and screaming.'

He looked at her.

'You shouldn't say that, Clara. Comparing a scream with — '

'A sudden desire to pray is what I mean. As for telling everybody — why should you? They know something's wrong. You can tell by these outbreaks of nerves and violence. Almost as if they feel they have to settle things somehow, to get things clear. To solve their little mysteries.' She looked at him. 'I may be wrong about all that. But I know I'm right when I say we should go on just as we always do, and if it comes, then it comes. If it's true we have only weeks left then make it a part of life as we've always loved it. Life is small things, hundreds — thousands — of small things. Little things that we love. Little things that we hate. When I come to look at it, it's like a pattern, a mosaic . . .'

Her voice trailed away, as if she had, all along, been persuading herself.

He waited. She began to cry a little. He went to her.

'You are right, dear. I won't tell what the false gods think.'

'Just one thing, Jim,' she said, turning

to him with a sudden anger. 'Don't let's have any more of this Jesus saves nonsense. In all my life and in most other people's lives we have had to watch suffering and God never did anything to save any living thing, and He won't start now. He's God. The Almighty. He made the universe and then left in it the attic to breed insects and people and everything else that comes to life from forgotten things. Kafka's compost. All right, so we must make the best of it . . . ' She broke off. He put his arms round her. She stiffened a little as if resenting his touch. Then she turned and went away from him. 'What about this bloody carnival? We must go on with it as if nothing is going to happen. The carnival. Where are my appointments?'

She went out. He sat down at his desk. He should write a sermon for Sunday.

About what?

Clara put on a sun-hat and went out. She crossed into Bell Wood, walked through to the river and watched the quiet water. Then she turned and went on under the trees, watching the powder colours of little flowers amongst the rocks by the water, then came out across the broad meadow to the edge of South Wood and the cottage and boat-shed by the river bend.

As she came near she saw George Heald sitting on the boat ramp, staring at the water as he munched a sandwich. He was a big man, his bare chest and arms all brown and shining from sun and sweat. She looked at him and stopped. After a while he knew she was there and looked round and saw her standing still on the grass. She smiled. He nodded and looked at the water again. Clara felt her heart beating and blood hot in her cheeks. The smile remained as she turned and walked to the garden gate. The sound of typing came out of the open door, muffled by heat. She tapped on the open door and went in. Bet was typing at the table. She sat back and smiled.

They had cups of tea and talked about people. It was rather flat.

Clara said, 'The bishop thinks . . . '

Bet said, 'I'm sure most people have got the idea now. There's enough guesswork being broadcast to put the wind up anybody.'

'I think it might be true.'

'If it happens, amen. It's not a thing worth bothering about, because it just can't be bothered about. Wait and see if it comes. It's always been a possibility, I suppose.'

'Mother used to have a saying from the war when they thought the Germans would invade. She said, 'If you've got to be raped, lie back and enjoy it.''

'I suppose one could?'

'I'd want to know the man, though.'

'Next you'd want to know it was a man you fancied. That's cheating.' They both laughed, then Bet said, 'How did Jim take the bishop's message?'

'I've left him to sort it out. He'll have to make up his own mind. How he'll manage to deal with the problem is hard to see. What he has to say is, 'God has had enough, and the whole universe will be treated to a live rerun of Sodom and Gomorrah, the Flood, apocalypse and the Bang in a new wrap-round experience.' Do you think I'm being facetious?'

'My dear husband, in the short time I had him, always called this place the Vale of Sad Banana.'

'Why?'

'Some kind of heavy sadness hit him when he first came here. But just before he went that last time, to Chile, there were wars everywhere and undercover civil wars and God knows what and he said then, 'It isn't just Rustum; it's everywhere. It's man's place, and he made it home.''

'Was he a sad man?'

'No. Very lively. Wicked, mischievous, lovely, loving.'

'Why didn't you marry again? It was a long time ago.'

'I didn't want to. My life centred on the girls.'

'But you must have done something,' Clara said. 'You were so young.'

'Clara, my mother was the only nun there ever was in our family, and she'd run through all the fleshpots by the time she left Father.'

Clara thought for a while.

'I envy you, Bet.'

'I'm a very lucky woman.'

There was a tap on the open door. George Heald stood there, looking in. Clara watched him.

'Farrow's ha'n't delivered that glue,' he said. 'It'll be needed nex' week.'

'I'll give them a ring, George,' Bet said. He nodded and went.

'There's a sexy beast,' Clara said, picking up her hat. 'Is he getting on all right with the famous boat?'

'He's a craftsman, but he's very shy. Makes him boorish.'

'Is he married?'

'I think he's separated. It's difficult to get him to talk about himself. He's all boats and wood and bowing and stressing. Just like Father. I never quite knew what he was talking about, either.'

'Show me the boat,' Clara said. 'I want to see everything I haven't really seen before.'

They went and saw the boat. George Heald went on working. The sweat was glistening on his chest when Clara stopped him to ask innocent questions. She did not understand the answers, but he turned his head away as each finished, so she murmured, 'I see,' as if she did and it made her thoughtful.

The women went.

'Satisfied?' Bet said as they walked along the bank.

'I don't really know anything about boats,' Clara said.

'With the man,' said Bet, and smiled.

Clara said nothing, then shrugged, then smiled and looked up.

'What are we here for?' she said. 'I don't know, but I have an awful feeling I haven't done it.' She frowned. 'Why on earth Sad Banana?'

'His potty vision. He said bananas growing in great hanging bunches, one over the other, always reminded him of the mop heads of sorrowing widows. And he said the sort of green colour was sad, too. Not fresh, but like mould.'

'Poetic — I suppose,' said Clara.

Sections of the male population in the village took a philosophical view of the coming of the End. Drink and be merry for tomorrow we die. The pub did roaring trade night after night. The only person who did not believe there would be no tomorrow was Jeff Wise, who would give no tick.

Knowing Bert resented this lack of convenience. He sat in the bar corner, glowered and spoke of strange things.

'Savin' it all fer God, 'e is. And when he gets there, God'll say to him, 'Ho there, sinnin' old publican, what you got in them bags?' and Jeff'll say, 'I brught me money fer to lay at yer feet,' and God'll say, 'I don't want none of thy money, Jeff. It smells o' sin and beer. Yo jest stick that up yer arse,' 'E'll say, 'and go to the bloody devil.' Arse-lickin' never did nobody no good,' he said, eyeing his emptying glass morosely.

But the general mood was such that money was crossing the bar in such quantities that Bert was watered as a by-product.

In a quiet moment one night, Jeff Wise said to Maud, 'I reckon the male part of Rustum will be drunk on Judgement Day.'

Maud said, 'If it doesn't come, they'll be broke till Christmas.'

It was dusk when she went into the barn. She stopped just inside, her heart beating fast. She could see lights spraying upwards from the end of the barn. The glow made her want to turn back and go.

A door opened. Light streamed out. She saw him in the light frame, a silhouette. He stood quite still.

'Clara?' he said.

She said nothing. He reached to one side. The lights went out. She saw his shadow come towards her and stop.

'It's so hot. I had to come out. Jim was called over to Hawley. Some other conference. All sorts of things are happening. Unexpectedly. It's very disturbing.'

'Would you like a drink?'

'Yes.'

They walked down to the office. He did not put a light on. He seemed to know she would not want it. He could see enough. It was not quite dark. He gave her a Scotch. They drank.

'I had an idea to surprise you,' he said,

in a dry, small voice. 'I would go into your part of the house and wait for you — in your bed. But then I thought — if you don't come back tonight . . . I had such burning shame, I wanted to run away and hide from myself — because you didn't come back to find me . . . '

She caught her breath as if catching a sob. He put his arm round and whispered in her ear. She listened tautly for a second or two, then relaxed and began to laugh, almost a giggle. He went on making her laugh while he gave her little kisses.

He was grateful she had come. The letter from his father had not been delivered until that evening by special delivery. His father had written:

I am ill. If anyone tells you I am very ill, take a dram for me and stay where you are. If you come all this way and I die it will waste the train fare. You may not be able to afford it when you read my will. I am sorry to leave you three illegitimate stepmothers, but you have always known how to cope with them . . .

The old man had died that afternoon, before Ian had been able to ring. He had died just ahead of the rest of humanity.

★   ★   ★

For the fourth night, the boy came silently into her bedroom, slipped on to the bed and cuddled tightly against her. She woke suddenly and felt him warm and firm against her body.

'Bobby. Bobby!' she said quietly and tried to break his hold on her. She could not. His head pressed between her breasts. She tried again, and suddenly he let go, turned over on to his back and lay there looking at her.

She sat up.

'What *is* the matter?' she said, and felt her heart beating fast. 'You're not still worried about going away?' He did not answer, but watched her, staring at her bosom as if he could see her heart beating under the silk. 'Are you? Who are these — people?'

He stared at her and began to smile slowly. She looked at his naked body and felt sharply apprehensive. He turned suddenly and grabbed her, pushing himself against her as if in desperation. He said nothing at all. She got his wrists, broke his hold on her and held his fists in front of his bent head.

'Bobby. Go back to bed. Something's upsetting you. Would you like to stay at school for a night or two — with the other boys. You won't be so frightened. Shall we try that?'

He stayed still, letting her hold his wrists together, head bent. Then he nodded, but did not look up. She let go. He stayed, head bent, half sitting. He started to cry and the tautness left his body. She put her arms round him and held him and felt a sense of loss, as if something had gone from the love between them. Things were changing. He was changing. He was not a little boy any more. She looked out at the moon going down from the high sky. Somehow the nights of the awful silences had ceased to feel so real to her. There were other fears lingering in the shadows of her mind. Fears of life, not death.

Bet took Bobby to school that morning with a case for the clothes he would need. She spoke to matron about the boy having been very restless at night. Matron said she would keep an eye on him.

The day of alarms began when she got back. She made coffee and took a mug across to George in the boat-shed.

'You must look for an assistant,' she said. 'You can't go on working all hours like this.'

'I'm beginning to get his shape,' he said, wiping his brow with the back of his forearm. His chest shone with sweat. He stared critically at the work he had done. 'I'll look out a boy I can teach.'

'You might have to have a girl,' she said, and laughed. 'You mustn't choose now.'

He shook his head.

'Not a girl. No. A boy is best.' He took the mug without looking at her. 'Thanks.' He drank and went on silently criticizing the way his work was matching with the old. He was not satisfied, she thought.

But then he probably never would be. Like her father. He had said of every boat he had built, 'That was the very best I could do — *then.*'

It was then that the phone rang. She took it in the little office, once against scattered with sketches and drawings, as it had been, thirty years before.

'Dr Richardson? Hallo! How are you, dear?'

'I keep myself very well, Betty. Know how. But look. Can you possibly come in and see me this morning?'

'I can. Yes, of course I will. When?'

'As soon as you can, dear. Something most important has happened and you are really the only one who can deal with it.'

'Yes, dear. I'll come now.'

'Thank you, my darling. Thank you.'

He sounded very old, she thought. Very tired, and yet somehow relieved. She went quickly, drove fast. There was an old carriage archway at the doctor's house leading to a yard behind. When she got out of the car she looked up at the rear steps which led up to his old surgery. He was standing at the open door, smiling down. She went up and kissed him.

'Now you go in the old waiting-room, my dear. You won't be disturbed.' He nodded, still smiling.

'But what — '

'Please, dear. Just go in.' He opened the door.

She went in. A woman stood by the window, looking at her. The door closed behind Bet; she stood quite still looking at the stranger.

'Roz,' she whispered. 'My little Roz.'

Roz went to her, arms out. For a long time the two women clung to each other, and then Roz stood back a little.

'Darling, Mummy,' she said. Her plump face was wet with tears. 'I'm still too fat, you see.' She turned away a moment, then used a small balled-up handkerchief. 'Mummy — I haven't come back. I must say that first. It's only fair.'

'How have you been? What's happened to you?'

'I'll tell you — in a moment. I've come for a very special purpose. I flew from Los Angeles. Stopped over at New York and took a day going up to see Liz. They all send their love. Dear old doctor sent up this coffee. Have some, Mummy, and sit down.'

'No, I don't want any coffee, dear. Just talk. Tell me.'

After a while, Roz spoke. 'When I left here I went to Dr Mason. He was head of the sect here. It was up in Norfolk, and I liked it. I want to be very quick, Mummy. No detailing. You mustn't mind. After a while Dr Mason took some of us to the main church in the States. I didn't like it. Razzamatazz. It was their style, not mine. Dr Mason knew it. Professor Hardwick from Princeton, was conducting experiments in psychic research. You know I was always a dreamer. Dr Mason detected some psychic value in me, and introduced me to the professor. I went to help him in his research laboratory at the university. He was impressed. I worked with him for five years, then went to a study group in Los Angeles, where I have lived since.'

She sipped some coffee. Bet watched and waited, patiently, but yearning.

'Three days ago, Mummy, two men

came to see me. They showed me their identification and asked me a good many questions about home, and about Bobby.'

'Bobby! Why? All that way off *about a schoolboy here?* Your son?'

'My son. Yes. I told them I had had an affair with a man my family never knew while I was still a schoolgirl. They pressed and pressed to find out about him. I told them no more than that, but I knew they'd come back and ask again. I then decided to come and see you.'

'You've come because of these men? And Bobby? But who were they?'

'They were from the Central Intelligence Agency, Mummy.'

Bet stayed silent, her mouth partly open. At last she found her voice.

'*About Bobby?*' Her voice was a whisper. 'But . . . '

She stopped and closed her lips. Roz watched.

'You're not as surprised as I thought, Mummy,' she said softly. 'Tell me.'

'There have been two men here from the Government, asking questions about Bobby. They asked around people who knew him. They came and saw me, but I pushed them off. They went away, but I've seen them back again. There's some story they are making a social survey, but I've been very watchful though they haven't come near. Now you say the CIA as well? What on earth is going on? Who was his father? Did you ever tell anyone?'

'No one — ever.' Roz shook her head. 'But because of these men, I've come back to tell you. You're the only one I could ever tell. Nobody else in the world would believe me. But you will.'

Bet got out her own handkerchief, closed her eyes and cried for a little while.

'The doctor sent this brandy, too, Mummy,' Roz said, and poured a little into a glass. 'Here.'

Bet, nodded, straightened and took a sip. 'Tell me, Roz.'

Roz had thought and rethought an opening during the hours on the planes, in the hours of waiting in the terminals, in the last hours on the train, until the words were perfect, but as she went to begin, she could not. She knew the words would not do, and had to be changed.

'You know I was always a terrible dreamer . . . ' It came out in a rush and stopped.

'All girls dream. You were a special one.'

'We dream of romance and we dream of sex. I used to dream for hours, making up, altering, making up again some more, stopping and altering because some part spoilt it, then going on over and over . . . I got lost in my dreams. Some were real. I could have orgasms from dreams sometimes once I grew a little older . . .

'It was that summer. It was very hot. I went out on my own in the evenings along by the river, in the wood. I had a little place under that overhanging rock, and the stars shone in the river and made everything look a little luminous, and the water sounds were gentle. It was a place so beautiful that time was quite lost there.

'Then one night, the boy came to me. He was the most beautiful boy I have ever seen. His beauty, like the river water, seemed to shine somehow in the twilight. He was so beautiful my whole body yearned for him and when he was with me I could feel his touch on my breasts, his lips on my face and the sounds of his voice caressing me like no other words I ever heard. But he never spoke words I had ever heard. I understood because they fondled me . . . Four nights he came to me there and went before I left. On the fifth night I knew I would be away and would not come, but I knew that whenever I would come again, he would be there, and so I was content.

'As the time passed I felt myself changing, I did not believe it could be real. In my mind, as the time went by, the beautiful boy had become more and more a part of a dream, which was the reason why he would always be there when I wanted him again.

'But when Bobby was born, my mind refused to understand what had happened. I knew too well that the beautiful boy was no earthly person. He was like one but totally separate from any earthly person. He could not even say the things an earthly person can say.

'In the years since, psychic research has helped me to grasp that something artificial can feel like reality. There is the possibility that with the strength of a loosely wandering mind suddenly encountering another, the force can be so immense that a conception of a living thing could be created from the force of the meeting.

'But it is an excuse, Mummy. The fact to my animal mind is that I do not know how or whence he came as a live being into this world. For me he is the product of a dream; of a wish so strong that he was created from a force of which I was, and still am, ignorant.

'Liz told me you fed him yourself, Mummy. Is that right? Did you?'

'Yes.'

'Did you not wonder how you managed such a thing?'

'I wanted to so much. Such things happen.'

'Perhaps. But it might have been that he demanded it. There is that way round, darling. It might have been essential to him to live.'

'Roz, darling, he is a normal boy. In every way. He has grown up normally, he has developed normally.'

'The men said he had an abnormal knowledge of mathematics.'

'Well, he's not the only child in the world like that.' She stood up, and so did her daughter. 'You must come back to him, Roz.'

'Mummy, you still don't understand. I can't. I must save myself. There are other children — not mine — but I have them. It's a small home we run. For children. It's important now. There is something going to happen which we can't stop. I must be with them. I had to tell you, Mummy, because of these men, but that's the only reason I felt I had to come and tell you. I know you're strong enough to take it. I never have been. I've had to smother it with something else. Something else to take me over, mind and all. I don't want to be alone any more to dream. I have to fight it away. I have to have other interests to take me over. I want no more of dreams.'

She kissed her mother.

'What do you mean, something is going to happen? To you?'

'You must have heard, Mummy. To all of us. That was the other reason why I came. To see you, tell you I love you, and go back to the children.'

'Do you really believe in this happening?'

'I've seen some of it already. I have seen small sections of disaster in my researches. Sections of events. Cuts. Yes. I'm sure it is going to happen. But I believe it will be so total and in such conditions that not a living thing will ever realize what is happening. You just won't know.'

She kissed once more, then Roz went, tall, quick, yet somehow reluctant. She looked round at the door, smiled, and turned away as the smile faded into grief, and she went.

After a half hour, Richardson shuffled in. Bet was sitting, thinking.

'Are you all right, Betty dear?'

'I've had a good cry, John. Now I'm all right.'

He put his hand on her shoulder and smiled and nodded at something a long way off, in some other world.

3

Driving home was painful for her. She kept thinking of his agony in the nights, and the pleading not to have to go back. There was nowhere in this world he could have feared to go back to. Yet he had never known any other. That was certain. He had been born in the orchard at Old Will's Cottage. He had been no foundling. She had seen Roz give birth from her beautiful body and known him intimately every day since. Then how did he know there was another place? Was it race memory that came with the father's seed?

But he had *seen* them, he said. He had *seen* them. Where? Near the house? At school?

She had not taken much notice before of his talking about people he had seen lurking to take him back. She had connected this with nightmare, but Roz's story suddenly brought the mysterious figures up into sudden, frightening close-up, so quick she could make out no details of them before they were gone.

The boy by the river. She could almost see him; like Bobby, beautiful, loving, caressing, but knowing no words, just sounds of love.

She was numbed by the ease with which the unexplained details of years ago suddenly fitted together. That strange stubbornness in the refusal to name a father; even to the point of saying there had never been one, and perhaps believing, right until the birth, that it must be a kind of phantom pregnancy, the fruit of a dream. But it had become real, and that week of unexplained fright Bet had seen, and put down to normal emotions of guilt, of shame, perhaps, had really been a real fear of the child itself. Then, suddenly, that strange escape which left no trail behind it, and the deliberate forsaking of her family in fear they might bring her back to the child she knew to be alien, perhaps a solid illusion which might suddenly prove hollow and fade into the dust of a dream in her arms.

Bet almost rammed another car, and shouted an apology out of the window.

The young driver raised two fingers and went on.

She stopped outside the town and walked by the river for a while. She cried a little. She had an awful feeling as if she were struggling for life in a flood, and all around her the material things of her life, which had been part of her, were being washed and torn away, floating debris on the storm water, rushing down to some unseen, destroyer sea.

She opened her eyes, shocked for a second at finding herself standing in the sun on the browning grass of the river bank, smelling the mud the river had left when it had shrunk into a fitful, sorrowing stream, its edge now out of reach of the bank. The heat was still, burning when she drew breath.

She turned away and went back to the car. She drove back quickly. The feeling of nightmare changed to an awful sorrow, as if at last she knew the world was going away from her and there was nothing she could do to stop it.

But when she parked by the boat-shed her emotion changed to anger at herself for believing that Bobby could be anything but a natural boy, and that there was nothing she could do to save herself from losing everything. She was angry at the CIA and the men snooping in the village . . .

She went into the boathouse. He was working. She watched his brown back shining as he strained to locate and fit a cleat. It looked as if he supported the whole boat on his broad shoulders, like a latterday Atlas. She watched his intense concentration and thought; he was a free man, wholly in his chosen work. He had no daughter who would suddenly appear after years of desertion and say that the love of the years for a boy was a sham; that he had never been a baby, nor a boy, but an unreal creature who had come from starseed and spawned in a dreamer's womb.

Frightened, she forced herself to see what he was doing. She bent close to him and peered under the wooden skeleton.

'What are you trying to do?' she said.

He jerked his head a little aside and without looking at her said, 'I've done it!'

175

He arched his back. His shoulder pushed against her breast. He leant away.

She straightened up. 'You looked as if you were having a job to do it. You must have an assistant. Bobby could help you.'

He drew his knees up and put his arms round them.

'He wants to farm,' he said. 'Likes animals. It's no good teachin' if he don't want to stick it.' He put a hand to his shoulder where her breast had touched and held it. He sat still, then got to his feet. She was standing close to him and looking away towards the stern-post. She could smell his sunbrowned skin. It was good. She knew he wanted to touch her and she wanted him to. The loneliness of fear needed companionship. She wanted him. But he turned away. She looked round to watch his powerful back. His arms were hanging, as if they had lost their strength, a rag in one hand, a chisel in the other. He dropped the chisel into a box and put a hand in his pocket, then pointed forwards with the rag in his hand.

'I'll have trouble — linin' up there. Difficult to see what he meant — there.'

He went further away from her deliberately, using the boat to protect him from being too near her.

She was angry again, and the feeling of loneliness became a great sadness.

She turned and went to the office door. She saw him look round, as if to watch where she was. She stopped. 'Have you any idea how long it might take to finish the boat? Roughly.'

'It's too soon yet,' he said. 'Without his drawin's I have to make it up, and that don't always fit in. So it's go back — start over again. No, I couldn't say yet. Couple of weeks I could, p'r'aps.'

She went into the office and shut the door. Through the glass side she saw him throw down the rag and go out on to the ramp and stand looking at the narrowing waters of the river, where they exposed the white mud of the far bank. She picked up the phone and dialled.

'Dr Hayes. It's Elizabeth Hicks speaking. I wanted to talk to you about my grandson, Miller, concerning his mathematical gift.

'There are two men in the village, and I

understand that they are waiting to interview him. They are from some government department. There are so many that are made up overnight to investigate something or the other. However, if they come to you wanting to see him, could you insist that I should be at any such interview? . . . Yes. Thank you.'

She put the phone back and stared out of the window. His trousers were on the ramp. He was in the deep water channel by the ramp, swimming as if he meant to get somewhere.

When she put the phone down loneliness seemed to come down over her like a blanket. She could not bear to be in that little place. She went out on to the ramp. He was sitting on the boards at the end, wet glistening on him. She wondered if he wore those little swim pants all the time. He was eating his lunch sandwiches, watching the river below the overhang of the woodwork.

She stopped. 'Would you like a drink?' she said.

He looked round, but at her feet, as if

178

he had never seen such slender sling-backs.

'Not now. Got a bellyful of river. Still fresh, though. Springs are still goin'. That's it. But they'll dry up if this goes on.'

She turned away towards the cottage and began to walk. He looked at her then and stopped eating. She looked back suddenly. He was looking at the feet again.

'I ordered the glue,' she said.

He nodded. She went on so angry at having stopped with such a feeble excuse as that. Glue! Like a silly schoolgirl. Glue! Of all things. Bloody glue!

She went into the cottage and poured a gin, then couldn't find the Cinzano. She was looking around the big kitchen when Clara came in.

'I've brought you the parish magazine, as I know you couldn't bear to be without the latest edition, dear,' Clara said.

'Of course,' Bet said. Glue, she thought. Bloody glue! Clara had been there when he'd asked. Glue. Clara and bloody glue. 'Thanks. Have a drink.'

Bet poured drinks using tonic water and squeezed lemon in as if she would strangle the fruit. Then she sat down. They drank. Bet watched Clara.

'I don't know what you've done,' said Bet, 'but it shows. I hope Jim hasn't noticed.'

'He won't,' Clara said. 'He's rushing about like a blue-arsed fly on these emergency committees, and they're not deciding what to do, you know. They can't decide what to do. It's as if God said we're all going to blow up. But He hasn't. God has never said anything. He gave up talking after he had to spend two days explaining to Noah what an ark was.'

Bet looked out through the open door. It was obvious the adultery that had troubled restless Clara had been committed and she was going to do it again, all over the place probably. She had been hidebound too long. Perhaps she should have stayed bound. But then — did it matter? Nobody knew now.

At a quarter to one, Bet told her to get out. Clara got up gathered up her little pile of magazines and said, 'Well, I only said, 'did you?' I mean the man is here — one just wonders. I didn't mean to pry.'

'I'm sorry, Clara. I'm upset this morning. My daughter came back — but she had to go again. I haven't seen her for so long.'

'Not Liz?' Clara softened.

'No. Little Roz. The one that — ran away. It upset me. But she had to go.'

'Oh, I am sorry, dear. Anything I can do?'

'No. I just want to be alone, I think. Till I get over it.'

'Of course.' Clara kissed her and went.

'Glue,' said Bet. 'Bloody glue.' She went to the phone. She didn't know what time it was in New Zealand. She didn't look it up in her little book where she had put down the times in Massachusetts and Auckland, NZ, at any time of day GMT with conversions for Summer Time.

She could not get through. International Exchange said they would call back. Bet got a sandwich, listened to the news and a women's programme. The exchange came back at two. Her caller was not available. Small local exchange said the subscriber was on holiday with his family, but the practice could take calls at his office in Auckland.

'Thanks, but no,' Bet said. Suddenly New Zealand was all of twelve thousand miles away in another world, remote, cold.

At one-forty, Sir Hugh rang from London.

'I'm up here again, sweetie. This Snark business. It keeps sending snippets of signals from different bits of the universe and we can't find where. Everybody's going potty. But it has been a bit overshadowed, of course. No. What I rang about, darling, is this. Now, I don't want you to be alarmed, my dear — yes, yes, I know that makes you worse — I mean, of course. You know me. Don't understand women. If I did I'd have hundreds and you my favourite — Yes, yes, dear. Well, look; it's a bit odd. One of the security departments has been asking questions about Bobby. Yes, well, they asked me about him as I'd known him since he was born — yes, I know some other buggers

182

did before down there, but this is higher-ups. I told them to get stuffed, but that roused their interest — probably wondering how to do it, eh? No. The way they looked at me after that, I'm beginning to feel I'm on some sort of suspect list, too. But you know this lot. They suspect anybody. Anyhow. Don't worry, but don't let them get at Bobby. Paint him with spots or something. I can't help as I can't get back for another couple of days. At school, is he? Well, they could help. You have? Oh, of course you would. Unique. Think of everything. Perhaps they could stuff him in quarantine or something. Eh? No. I think it's to do with the Snark. Ian. The maths. You know. Well, I must trot, sweetie. I'll look in as soon as I get back. Take care. Love. Bye-bye.'

At least, she had installed the warning system with Dr Hayes at school. There was really nothing to do but wait.

But at three-twenty-five, the two men came again. Bet was in the garden, picking herbs, and wore big dark sunglasses. She kept them on. The men sat on a seat made out of an old boat engine cover. She sat on a garden roller, facing them. The fair man began to talk.

'Let's cut the prologue,' Bet said, cutting him short. 'What do you want this time?'

The fair man began again with a cold skirting round of what he wanted. Bet looked away.

'Perhaps I could put it less formally,' said the dark man, leaning forward.

She looked at him quizzically.

'Our government is wiser and wishes to be wiser,' said the dark man, 'and it must disturb whatever it can in order to find out something which, when it is found out, turns out to be something it didn't want to know. As now. We — '

'This is not the case — ' the fair man began.

Bet held up a hand. 'Let him go on, please.'

'Briefly, Intelligence — I apologize for the pretension — was puzzled some years ago by what are popularly known as flying saucers. Some landings of actual people were reported and treated by Intelligence as a load of cock and bull. However, some other landings were recently reported, so the whole thing has come up again.

'Now your grandson has caused more than some surprise in high places by an extraordinary mathematical genius which is so far above the grasp of Government Intelligence — '

'I would — ' said the fair man angrily.

'You would not,' said Bet. 'I am beginning to understand. Please go on.'

' — that some nut in the department said he had to be extra-terrestrial in origin, because some gossip in the same department knew Mr Brown, who lives in this village and remembers a baby being born in an orchard. Briefly, Mrs Hicks, the case is they think your daughter, who was too young to know what was happening, was taken one night by a handsome Saucerian who implanted his alien seed in your daughter's womb, then cast a spell of forgetfulness on her so that she would not remember her lover, and so an alien was born and you were magicked into receiving this child so that when your frightened daughter ran away you were given the power to suckle the infant by hypnosis, which is the only thing the biology professors could come up with.

'What we are here for, then, is to persuade you to agree that this load of wallop is the truth.'

The fair man was dead still, unable to object by any vocal means, so intense was his fury.

Bet smiled.

'I am very grateful to you for putting it so clearly,' she said. 'However, I can assure you that my daughter is far from being an idiot child, in fact, after leaving here she spent several years helping research at Princeton University in America. She is, however, a very loyal person and that is why she has not told anyone who her lover was. Probably, she found that he was married. I wonder the department did not think averagely enough to hit on that.

'As for my abundance of milk on several occasions in my life, it is just that I am an exceptionally good cow. I have suckled several children in this village, and when my daughter left, I was only 32 at the time. My secret was, I used herbs, of which I know a good deal, to produce the power to nurse him, which I did.

'As you have been so forthright, and as you'll find out, anyhow, I met my daughter this morning for a short time, and she told me she had been worried by some fatuous visits she had had from the CIA. If this hunt for an alien child has spread to the United States it must be because of the lack of intelligence being shown by our Intelligence Department here. If you and the CIA want to amuse yourselves with fairy-tales, please leave me and my grandson right out of it. If you will not I shall have no alternative but to apply to have him made a ward of court to protect him against persecution by Intelligence officers.'

The dark man stood up.

'You have my support, Mrs Hicks. In fact, unknown to my superior here I have resigned my position, with all the discomforts that will assure me for some considerable time to come, and I have done it because I am sick of this sort of witch hunt and evil innuendo.' He turned to his partner. 'I am sorry I didn't tell you exactly what I had done, but God knows, you asked for it.'

The fair man got up, raised his eyebrows, nodded briefly to Bet, then walked out of the garden, dignified as a cashiered guardsman.

Bet said, 'Come and have a drink.'

'Thank you. Just one. I need just one.' He followed her inside. 'The ward of court idea is good, but it won't work, you know.'

'I'm not surprised,' she said. 'I only thought of it then.'

'You fight, don't you?'

'When it is worth fighting for.'

A car horn tooted twice. The official car was by the gate.

'I'll run you back,' Bet said. 'You don't want to row all the way back.'

'He wouldn't row. It would be frozen silence. Anyway, I have a friend in the village.' He went out on to the path and made a scrub-out sign with his hands.

The car started off towards the road. The dark man turned back to the cottage. From the ramp, George looked up from emptying wood shavings into a bunker. He closed the lid with a bang and went back to the workshop. The ex-inquisitor went back into the cottage.

'Supposing the boy was tainted in some way,' Bet said. 'What would they do?'

'Put him in a laboratory and analyse everything with every known electronic analyser. Study everything, face to faeces. He would become an exhibit in a closed circuit of superbrains. Do you know what the weakness of the superbrain is? It can't recognize a fool. They ask questions. Who did build Stonehenge? What was it? A computer? An astronomical wonder of the time? Or was it a Druid's folly? Why did they go so many miles to get the stone when there was a variety of stone almost on the doorstep? Did they know the other stones might go to clay and disappear back into the earth and finally end up making newsprint at the end of a hundredth recycling, for *The Times*? How did they know? Who were they? But our egghead can't answer any of that. They hunt around finding small boys who can do maths better than they can and assume at once there's something alien about him.'

'Is that the only thing that made them go to all this trouble? You, the CIA and God knows who else, all because he can work out the trajectory of a cricket ball and make allowance for the wind?'

'He can do it with the bloody stars, Mrs Hicks. That's what jerked them out of the buttoned upholstery. The boy's headmaster took him to town and the dinosaurs took fright.'

'But my father could work out all the geometry for an entirely new boat, all the mathematics, intersection shapes, dimensions, timber sizes and everything else in his head. The only time he made drawings was when looking for artistically satisfying curves, and then, having found one on paper, he usually elaborated it into a naked overbusty lady. Then he chucked it in the wastebasket, but remembered the curve exactly.

'One of my twin daughters could read at 3, and could read anything at 5. She not only read, but she remembered and could talk about it. By the time she was

11 she could talk on almost any subject and her reading scope was unbelievable. Then she went to an upper school, and her interest became attracted away to boys, and clothes, and all that early genius faded and she became a normal girl, and her reading turned to oceans of romance and somehow the genius of the early years seemed to fade away, or perhaps it changed into something else. But it went.'

'I know, Mrs Hicks. I know. But I am on your side. What I've done this afternoon is give you a lot more time. I've blown the gaff. You know what they're up to, and probably now any further action will have to be handed over to a quite different department. Instead of sending people like us to try and get in under the back door, they'll have to consult with you. It'll take them a while to decide. They may not even decide before the world comes to its predicted end next Tuesday week, I understand. However, the Indians said last Tuesday week, so perhaps we've had it already. In the meantime, thank you for the drink, Mrs Hicks. I am very glad to have met you. I shall spend the remaining days in the study of pew end carvings.'

The first interesting shapings he had in mind was the baker's bosom. He walked back into the village, not caring at all if the world ended, so long as it was after he got to the bakery.

4

She could not stay in the cottage, but went out and walked along by the river. She searched the wood for the place of the overhanging rock, the enchanted place by the river, but could not find it. There was a place she thought must have been it, but then, walking on, found another, different place and, further, yet another. She walked a long way beyond the wood before she turned back. In the fields it was hot and still, close to the river it felt cooler, but only by a little.

She felt sweat trickle down between her breasts and mopped her neck with a little handkerchief, already wet. She stopped in one of the secret places by the stream and sat down on a rock to rest. It was too hot. She felt closed in by heat. She slipped off her open shirt, then her bra, then put back the shirt loosely and flapped the edges to cool herself. It made her feel cooler.

She could see the stars moving in a slow dance on the sluggish water, and then looked round behind her, suddenly apprehensive, as if the magic boy might be there behind her, come to tell her with his love sounds how he had loved little Roz, and how he wanted her and would search everywhere until he found her again — and suddenly she would hear a sound and see a frog croaking on a stone in the quiet water. Bloody fairy-tales. Frogs and princes and beautiful boys and glue and Clara chattering like a laughing head while her body was away with a man, or a beautiful boy, or a frog . . .

It was almost dark, but the yellow moon lay like a cheese rind on the eastern hills. There were no lights on in the cottage or the boat-shed. He had gone home. The world was quiet. She was alone. She wanted to cry, and was angry to be weak.

She went into the cottage. She had left

the door open when she had gone out. She did not shut it. It was too hot. She left the light off. She stood by the table. She wanted to cry again. Then suddenly she could smell his sunburned skin. She half turned as he tried to get hold of her. He caught hold of the open shirt and ripped it backwards to keep her from getting away. She let it come off and started forward. He went after her and caught her round the middle. She struggled and kicked back. His arms eased slightly. She used all her strength to get away, and almost succeeded, but he changed his hold and she turned to him as his arms locked round her. She felt her bare breasts pressed against his sweating chest and for an instant felt she would let go. He tried to kiss her. She turned her head to one side.

'No! No, you fool! You fool!'

She brought her knee up. His grip broke. He went back, head lowering as he half doubled up. She saw the handle of a copper frying-pan on the cold stove, snatched it, swung it up and smashed it down on his head. She meant it to hurt, and made to hit him again, but the pan made a sound. It went 'Dong!' She suddenly stayed still. There was something absurdly funny in that noise. It made the whole fury of the scene change face like putting on a clown's red nose. She let the pan fall to the table, and began to laugh. She laughed wildly. She saw him squatting on the floor, stunned. She went to him, took his head and pressed it against her belly and laughed, tears running down her face.

Suddenly he took his head from her embrace and bent right down. He kissed her bare feet, one after the other, then turned on all fours like a dog, jumped up and went quickly out of the door, striking the doorpost with his shoulder so hard it half turned him in the opening. He went off into the darkness.

She went to the door and looked out, but could not see him. She called his name, but there was no answer. She did not hear him any more.

She went back in, closed the door and bolted it, then went upstairs in the dusky light, undoing her skirt as she went. She reached her room and threw herself on to the bed and cried into the pillow. She was sad, hurt and lonely. She cried until there was no passion left in her, and she fell into a sleep of exhaustion.

She awoke suddenly. The room was bright with moonlight. She sat up, heart beating fast, and looked up at the ceiling. Then she got up, went to the door and ran down the stairs, naked like a ghost crossing the moonbeams. She fought with the bolts as if she had never used them before, and pulled the halves of the door wide open. She went out on to the path and stood there, staring at the sky.

The silence was on. Nothing in the world moved. She did not see him sitting there with his legs out on the ground, his back against the wall. He got up, slowly, silently and stood just behind her, and like her, stared up at the awful, silent sky.

She did not look round and suddenly reached back with her hand and gripped his, as if she could see him there. They stood there, that one small grip seeming to hold them to all life.

The silence stayed. Nothing in the

world moved any more. She felt the earth was beginning to fall, gathering speed in a silent drop down into empty space; the whole vast mass of the earth was falling.

She grasped his hand with all her strength, as if it were the last thing in all life there was to hold to. And still the awful silence lasted.

Then from the wood there was a sound. The short, frightened cry of an owl, and then, as if the sound released all life, the dry leaves on the trees began to move again in the night air, and the murmur of the river came again, and all the sounds of the woods and the fields came back in the heat.

She looked at him, her eyes rimmed with sudden tears. He made as if to speak, but could not make a sound. They stood still a long time, frightened the world might still die, as if their own lives would not quite come back to them.

★   ★   ★

They stood at the window, looking out on the village street. Nothing moved anywhere. The world held its breath. He

197

stood by the bed, watching her naked body, and tried to ignore the petrifying silence and hold his frightened mind on to her beauty. Fat, yet, but of the Reubens kind; the Rape of the Sabines — God! What if it didn't go on? What if the silence stayed forever?

The sparkle of a new sweat showed as the moonlight shone on his face; the sweat not of heat, but of fear. Funk. The holding of the heart in a clamp of funk.

But she was beautiful. Oh yes . . .

Then faintly the world rustled, and gradually came awake again. It was over. Life went on.

'Annie,' he said, 'have you ever thought of marrying?'

She turned and looked at him.

'Are you seriously thinking of a future?' she said, huskily.

'With you — yes.'

She laughed. It was a strained, almost desperate sound at first, but eased and became more natural towards its end.

'You do choose the occasion, don't you? Kiss my hand or something.'

He took her in his arms once more.

'Haven't you chucked your job?' she said.

'I'll find another. I am in the Establishment. They won't let me go free. There'll be another offer.'

'You talk as if nothing is happening!' She searched his face with disbelief.

'There's always been a danger that one day the whole bloody lot would blow up. People didn't stop because of it. No point in stopping now. I want to be with you if it goes on. I want to be with you if it ends.'

* * *

Maud stayed lying on the bed, staring at the ceiling. He went to the window. It was natural to want to see out — to *know* . . .

When it ended she suddenly went flaccid. Her head rolled sideways on the pillow as if the sudden release of tension had killed her. He went and sat on the bed and wiped her brow with his handkerchief. With his relief a love for her welled in him. He wanted to say something that would warm her for him.

Minutes passed as he sat there and she lay placid.

'It's over, Maud. With Annie. It's over.' She came to life. Her head rolled back on the pillow so she could see him. Her eyes searched his face. Slowly he began to smile a little.

'That's 'cos there's another man for her, Jeff. I know.'

She turned over and closed her eyes, facing away from him.

★ ★ ★

'I don't want to,' she said.

'Look, let me show you — put you in the mood so you want to, Maxie.'

'I don't want. I told you I don't want to. No! No! Don't do that! Take me home. I want to go home!'

'Look, Maxine, I . . . '

The universe intervened. He looked up through the back window, then opened the door and scrambled out and stood by the car staring up at the sky showing in the brakes between the trees. She got out of the other door, fumbling to do up her dress. Then she looked upwards, and began to run. He said nothing but stood staring up. She ran back up the track to the road, and then when she came out of the trees under the sky and found the silence all round her. She stopped, bent her head and clapped her hands over her ears, though there was no sound in all the world for them to hear. She stayed there, sobbing almost silently until the sound had returned but her hands were too tight clamped for her to hear it.

The car came up beside her. He got out and touched her. She started.

'I'll take you home,' he said, then took her hands from her ears. 'Get in, Maxie. I'll take you back. Home.'

She cried all the way back, sniffing, looking out of the window. He kept saying he was sorry, but he was angry. At the house she said nothing, just got out and went to the house. He drove off.

She used her key and ran into the hall. The lights were on. Mr Barnes was standing there in his dressing-gown, staring at her. Her heart quailed. She wanted to turn and run out again.

'Thank God you're back, darling!' he said, and took her in his arms.

She cried loudly then.

★   ★   ★

Jim stopped the car and got out. He looked round the world of the open sky and wondered why it had died. Why were there no screams around him, no flames, no holocaust? He could not understand why not. He could not understand anything. Comprehension had all gone from him. This was something that did not belong to his world.

Then suddenly the earth moved, he heard sounds, he heard his heart pounding inside him and breathed deeply to calm it. The heat came back like a wave from an opened oven. He took off his jacket and flung it into the car, eased his collar with a finger, then unfastened it and took it off. He threw it into the car, then got back in behind the wheel and began to pray, then stopped; something he could not remember ever doing before.

Pray to whom? If the universe was

ending as a form of life he knew, what good could prayer do?

The sweat was running on his face. 'Forgive me,' he muttered and restarted the engine.

When he went into the vicarage it was quiet and dark. He went into his study and drank a small brandy without putting the light on, then went upstairs to the bedroom. It was empty. He looked at the path of moonlight lying across the smooth cover of the bed, then turned and went downstairs. He washed up the brandy glass in the kitchen, dried it carefully, then took it back and put it in its place in the study. He made sure he had left nothing behind, then left the house, his jacket over his arm, his collar in his hand, and drove away.

He slept in the car as much as he could, and did not come back to the vicarage until ten in the morning. Clara was there washing some small things in the kitchen. He kissed her.

'All night sitting, dear,' he said. 'Wondering what to do for the best.'

★　★　★

The hiatus had been the longest; 57.4524 seconds; enough to terrify the sophisticated.

In Rustum, the people went to sleep again eventually, to dream of all the things they knew coming to an end. But by morning, the sun came up as usual, and the heat came back, as usual, and the broadcasts warned of forest and grass fires from careless cigarette smokers and picnickers, and spoke, almost deliberately, of political changes in the United States, a coup in Africa, a counter-revolution in Guatemala, and ended with what records the weather was breaking; in the course of which it mentioned in passing that there had been another time lapse overnight, as if making more of it might spoil the sales of soap, breakfast cereals or BBC programme publications.

The Cabinet met in the capital, still united with other governments in not knowing how to handle such a situation.

Science admitted, with some sadness, 'It seems that there must be a bit more to gravity than we have hitherto supposed.'

'That must be true of everything we

think we know about,' said the Prime Minister, even sadder and obviously wiser.

'Life seems to be a gradual process of finding out what we don't know,' said the Home Secretary, shaking his head.

'The point I was going to make,' said Science, asperity marking his disapproval at having been interrupted, 'is that, according to what we knew till now, during fifty-seven seconds, everything should have fallen off the earth.'

'There must be a cohesion factor,' said Foreign, who had for years past been trying to find such a factor among foreign governments. 'Something holding it together as well as holding it down.'

'The atmosphere should have been chucked off as well!'

'Wouldn't the RPM hold something together?' said the Home Secretary.

'Where is this discussion leading?' asked Environment irritably.

'But to the grave,' said Science. 'The big one, up there in the sky.'

Levity produced a silence followed by a rustle of fidgets.

'You have the details of other government thinking before you,' said the Prime Minister. 'Is there any suggestion there which could help us?'

The Home Secretary shook his head, the others followed.

Of the Establishment the two notables who contributed but little to general secret discussions were the Archbishops of Canterbury and York, who, representing their bishops and the wide body of the clergy, were faced with the undoubted fact that ninety per cent of people did not much care about the idea of God saving them after He had slaughtered them untimely.

But everywhere, as the sun came up, or the night came down on time, and everything was still where it had been last night and for the last thousand nights, general fear withdrew into the wings.

The truth was, Doom was much too big to believe.

9

1

The boy came back just after four in the afternoon. The split door was open. He leant his back against it, hands behind him, and watched her at the table, typing. She looked up and saw him, then sat back in her chair without taking her eyes off him. Neither spoke. It was as if knowledge had made strangers of them.

The silence grew long. He shifted uneasily.

'I had to come back. I had to.'

She got up and went to the phone on the wall, watching him as she took it off and put her finger to the dial.

'You won't ring the school?' he said suddenly alarmed.

'I have to,' she said. 'I don't want them to think you're lost.' She rang through and explained he had come home and would stay the night now he was here.

She turned round, looked at him again, then went and switched on the kettle.

He came up to put his arms round her. She took his hands and put them back to his sides.

'Why did you come back? Have you seen these people again?'

'Yes.'

'At the school?'

'Yes.'

'Who are they?'

'I don't know.'

'Where do you see them?'

'They come in the night.'

'How?'

'I don't know. I look round and they're there.'

'How do they speak to you?'

'With voices.'

'Ordinary voices?'

'No. They don't come from here. You knew that, didn't you?' He watched her with a strange excitement shining in his eyes. 'How did you find out?'

'I was told.'

'Are you frightened of them?'

He hesitated, then shook his head. 'No.

But I don't like them. They're cold. They speak to me as if they command. I hate it. I don't want them to come again, Liz darling. I want them to keep away.'

'I love you, Bobby, and I don't want you to be frightened, but what can I do when I've never seen them?'

'You always do something, Lizzie, you always do something.'

She made tea. He stood watching her, trying to read what she was thinking from her actions. She got cake out of the wall cupboard. He knew she was just doing everything just to do it and not speak. That made him uneasy to the point of alarm.

'Don't make me go away, Liz!'

She turned and put down the cake. She stared at him for a moment, and then she went and took him in her arms as if nothing had happened to make them strangers.

'How did you get back?'

She got bread and butter, jam and cake, and poured the tea, while he said he had walked a way, then got a lift, then walked again. It was so hot he had sat on the bank a lot under the hedge where he found one.

'I've got to see Uncle Hugh and Ian,' he said suddenly, with cake halfway to his mouth.

'Uncle Hugh's away I think, but Ian's there. Why do you want to see them?'

'It's about maths,' he said and went on eating cake. 'Can I ring them? Do you mind?'

'Of course not. So long as they don't mind.'

★　★　★

She sat under the trees by the launching ramp, reading proofs. The old bench seat was polished with the sittings of angling philosophers, girls excitedly gossiping, or ruing unfaithful swains; Tom sitting there alone, smoking his pipe, sad at the girls' going until his head filled with some new boat.

In those days, through all those years it had seemed the world would go on forever. Perhaps it did seem it would, until the Silence came; then it didn't.

210

He came quietly, his jacket, hooked on a finger, slung over his shoulder; his tie loose his collar undone. She looked up and smiled. He kissed her. He gathered up proof sheets from the seat beside her. He sat down.

'George gone?'

'He hasn't turned up today. Funny man. I can't really make him out. Last night — when it came — ' She paused as if drying up at the memory ' — I went outside. I felt I should suffocate inside. He was sitting outside with his back up against the wall. Then when he saw I was upset and frightened he put his arms round me, then he waited to make sure I was all right, then just went. I haven't seen him since.'

'A grim and silent man; a melancholy man, remote from all,' he said, wiping his face with a handkerchief. 'Wasn't that The House of Usher? I can't remember now.'

'What's it like in town?'

He gave a short laugh. 'Dreadful! Everybody talks about nothing. There's this sort of no-tomorrow outlook, and yet it won't fix because everybody's scared there might be. Conscience is a terrible enemy. I wish I'd never come across it. I think it comes from stern parents and tough public schools. They beat guilt into you.' He, too, was talking to fend off something that worried him. Then he said it. 'Bobby's up with Ian.'

'Yes. He said he was going. Did you see him?'

'Yes. I was there. He got sent off cricket again. Fell on the wicket. I think he plays the clown. Do you know about — his *people*?'

'Yes. He's told me. He's seen them several times over the last fortnight or three weeks. When did he tell you?'

'Just now, Bet dear. He just let everything go. I can't imagine he told you all of it.'

'He said the people had been talking to him.'

'Did he tell you what about?'

'No.'

He sighed. 'He came up really because he and Ian talked a lot of the maths that finally went into Snark. That was quite a while back. Three years, I suppose. Extraordinary boy, Bet dear. Anyhow, he came because he thinks he can bring the bloody thing back into control because of a twist in the earlier figures. Well, he might. He might not. Who cares now? He sensed I felt like that though I didn't say it to him, and he went on to tell us what these people of his told him.'

'*You* believe in these people?' She watched him.

'I do. Yes. I think it was the intensity of his feeling. The way he spoke he didn't care whether we believed or not, and that convinced me. He wasn't trying to convince us. He was trying to find a way of calming himself over it. Alien people, Bet. There must be some, somewhere. Like us or not. We're this shape because this shape and the organ arrangements permit us to live in these conditions of essential gasses, but there could be others without number who can live in quite different arrangements. The idea that God created man in His own image must be the Great Blasphemy. If the Old Man finally turned out to be anything like me

I'd say, 'For Christ's sake, let me out of here!'

'But Bobby's people — yes. I believe what he said to us just now.'

'Let me interrupt for a moment, Hugh. The men have gone. The Intelligence men.'

'You got rid of them? Clever girl.'

'But, Hugh, they came because they had worked something out about Bobby. It was outlandish, it was absurd on the face of it, but it was right in every detail.'

'*What* was right?'

'Roz came yesterday.'

'Roz? After all this time? Oh, Bet my love, that must have been great for you.'

She told him what had happened between them. He put his hand on hers and stayed silent.

After a while she said, 'Does Bobby know anything about — what's happening?'

'Yes, yes. The alien people have told him. It seems they're refugees. Their planet has gone — or become uninhabitable. They're floating about in what we call a space fleet a long way off — waiting.'

'To see what happens?'

'Well — he says they're waiting to come here.'

'But if this earth is going as well — or do you mean they think it isn't?'

'They've told Bobby they know it won't go. They have the tracks of this cataclysm and we're right out of it, but we're getting the vibrations from it. The result of that, they reckon, is to shake the system out of balance but that it would recover in about a thousand years.'

He laughed. So did she.

'Well, it's a relief,' she said. 'Only a thousand years!'

'That's right, sweetie. Shall I book seats for the great comeback?'

Hugh looked at the sky. Bet saw the river cease to run sluggish down its now narrow channel and begin to swirl in small, lazy whorls. The birds became silent. The wind died.

He stood up, and in another second so did she. Their hands linked together tightly. The world stopped. There was no sense of passing time, just an absolute suspension, no murmur of warm wind, no creak of an insect, no beat of a heart; no life moved at all.

A rustle came back, then a scuttering amongst the leaves as birds, alarmed, beat about their nests as if preparing for a last defence of their young. The river smoothed out the whorls of weedy disturbance and began to run sluggishly again.

Hugh let his breath go.

'It wasn't so long,' he said. 'Not that time.'

★   ★   ★

In the village the street died in a frozen frame of film. Everyone was still, waiting. No car engine turned; every one was stopped so that men could listen. Everyone was listening for the sound of apocalypse coming across the silent sky.

When life came back, action returned slowly. People began to move, then be still again to listen. Everybody thought there would be sound when the final moment came; but when they listened, there was no sound in the world.

The bar was quiet. Men stood about, talking about the silence. There was a tense, strained air in the room. Talk came in spasms.

'If it is the end of the bloody world, then what can we do about it? Nothing!'

Pause.

'There might be something. I thought of asking Doc Ritchie. He knows all about bloody planets and, God knows, he has to because of his rockets and stuff.'

Pause.

'If you asks me, he might be arf the cause, shootin' bloody rockets up there. You think of all them bloody rockets and saturlites and shit all clattering round the sky like buckets on a string, it's bound to upset things, ain't it? They shoulda left well alone, they should. All brain and no bloody sense, that's what it is.'

Pause.

'We could ask him anyway. He might know what to do.'

'If it's the end of the bloody world there's nothin' you can do. You just got to wait fer it. That's all.'

'It's no good to run, is it? I mean, what

you're runnin' on's gonner bust up same time as you.'

Pause.

'Well, anyhow, Ritchie'll know more'n we do. So would Rawley. We could arsk them. I mean, they couldn't know less than what we do. I'm goin' up there. Who's comin'?'

Several decided to go.

'After all,' Jeff Wise agreed, 'Ritchie couldn't know less than this lot.'

'It's never happened in the daytime before,' Maud said, coming up to him.

'It has now.'

'It didn't seem so bad, somehow, not in daylight.'

'It freezes my guts any bloody time! I wonder what the hell it really is?'

★　★　★

They heard Brett shouting; a bull voice bawling through his open cottage door. Audie Drift was passing up the street, coming from the shop. She stopped and turned. The voice was beginning to sound desperate. She turned and went to the

218

Brett's cottage, knocked on the door.

'Are you all right, Mr Brett? Mr Brett!' She went in. 'Mr Brett!'

'I'm here. I can't get up the bloody stairs. She don't answer. She usually comes down — like now.'

'Would you like me to go up? I'll go if you like, just in case she's been taken ill or something.'

She went up. Flo was dead. She had taken dozens of aspirin. She still had the bottle in her hand, two or three tablets lying on her chest, as if she had swallowed in a hurry.

'Is she all right?' Brett called up.

'No. Just a minute — I'll come down.'

She put Flo a little straighter and pulled the sheet over her face, then she went down to Brett.

'I must get a doctor,' she said. 'Poor Flo is dead. She's taken a lot of aspirins.'

He looked stunned.

'She must a bin frightened of it,' he mumbled.

'I don't think she was ever frightened of anything like that,' Audie said. 'I think it was because she couldn't bring herself to

219

go out any more.'

She walked out. 'I'll phone doctor.'

2

'Who the hell's that?' Clara hissed.

'Hang on' Ian Ritchie said. He went to the door and clicked on a television screen. 'Looks like a deputation coming into the barn.' He turned round.

She started gathering her bag and gloves off the table.

'I must get out of here, Ian! Is there a back door?'

'There's a fire door. I'll show you.'

When he came back to the office door the tube showed quite a crowd, all men, gathered in the barn. He switched if off and opened the door.

There were a lot of questions being shouted from different parts of the crowd.

Ritchie held up his hands for quiet. When the shouting died to a mumble he vaulted up on to a hay platform and stood up. The evening sun slanted in at the great doors of the barn, and the faces gathered at the hay platform were painted in weird shadows by the reflection of golden light.

'First of all, brothers, it ain't my fault.' Somebody laughed. Others joined in, and then there was quiet again. 'Now what's the matter?' He pointed to the postman. 'Say,' he said.

'We thought you might know what's goin' on. You know — these sorts of — stops. There was another one an hour back. What is it?'

'*Is* it the end of the world?' came a cry from the back.

'I don't know,' said Ritchie. 'If it is, we'll have to put up with it.' Somebody laughed, then stopped. There was a pause. It was tense and quiet in the great cathedral. 'This world has ended before,' Ritchie said. 'We know of animals that existed once; a lot of different animals who all — suddenly — died. We don't know why. We've had a lot of guesses, but nothing has really solved the mystery of what happened. Dinosaurs and all their mates just stopped living quite suddenly. We have guessed at floods, eruptions, all sorts of damnation but could never visualize anything big enough to have ended a whole world of creatures. But it happened. It's probably happened several times. We don't know. But if it's any consolation to you lot, those disasters, however great, didn't destroy life.

'The Almighty didn't come wading through the stars and pick up Earth and say, 'I overdid that; I'd better make some more animals,' and then start moulding the clay all over again. No. The Old Man didn't come a second time. There was quite enough life left after the holocaust to get everything going again and make us a world as we've got it now. Maybe it'll happen again. Maybe it won't. But sure as hell it's no damn good wasting your time wondering. I know it's frightening, but life is frightening. It's frightening *all* the time, if you like to stop and think about it all the time, but you don't, do you? So don't start now.'

★　★　★

Clara stopped suddenly. Just round the corner of the barn wall, Miss Wainwright had stopped. The two women looked at each other, both colouring slightly from the heat as if each had not quite felt it so hot before.

'I — feel I'm hiding,' Miss Wainwright said, breathless. 'A lot of the men suddenly came up the lane and I — I just turned and came up here. I don't know what's the matter with me, really I don't. I'm getting so I can hardly face anybody. Oh dear!'

'I'll walk with you,' Clara said, relieved. 'Are you going home?'

'Yes, I suppose ... I hardly know where I am going now. Everything is so *strange*. I mean — what time is it? They won't give the time on the wireless any more. They say it's because it's wrong. But how can time be wrong? It's only a few seconds, isn't it? What does it matter? I don't really care what the time is, so long as they *say* it, or the pips or Big Ben. It's all so strange.'

'We can have our own time, by the sun. It's only a hundred years since everybody

223

had the same time in the country.'

'Suppose the sun stops? Suppose that stops next? What should we do?'

'Wait till it goes again, I suppose,' Clara said shortly. Miss Wainwright was making her nervous about all sorts of things.

* * *

Mr Barnes stared at his daughter in alarm and anger.

'Men?' he said. 'What sort of men?'

'I don't know. They were strange altogether.'

'Did they speak to you?'

'No, they — watched me. It was so odd I wanted to run.'

'Where was this.'

'Bell Wood. Coming down by the river. You know — the path. It's cooler.'

'I'll get the police to look into it.'

'Don't do that, dear,' said Mrs Barnes with unexpected courage.

'Why not?'

'They didn't interfere with her. They just looked at her.'

'She said they were strange-looking men.'

'Yes. That's what I mean. You know Sir Hugh Rawley's daughters are at Old Will's Cottage now and they have rather odd artist friends.'

Unusually, Mr Barnes considered the point his wife was making.

'Oh, I see,' he said and turned to his daughter again. 'Where were they exactly?'

'By the river bend. As Mummy says, they could have come out of Old Will's Orchard — you know, at the end of the garden there.'

'What do you mean by strange? Dirty? Gipsy?'

'No. Not dirty at all. I can't really explain. I suppose it was the caftans they had on. Very shiny, gold — '

'Caftans?' said Mrs Barnes. 'Then definitely artist friends.' She discarded the problem and got on with her knitting.

'I will get the police if you're worried?'

'No, Daddy. I'm not worried. I just mentioned it because they were — rather

225

strange, staring like that — Please don't worry.'

★ ★ ★

'I'm hanged if I understand it,' the vicar said. 'The people seem to know it will happen, but they don't believe it will end their lives.'

'But it's a bloody — pardon — difficult thing to stop and look at your workshop and your tools and at the job that's got to be out by Saturday, and the letter from the Bank, and then to think to yourself, 'Tomorrow there will be nothing at all,' said Gage. 'That it could all stop, vanish, be nothing. It's not possible, is it? It's exciting to think of things like that, but when I comes to the actual *believing* you won't even be here in an hour's time — well it just doesn't work, does it?'

Mrs Olney came into the vestry.

'I think you ought to go along, vicar. Flo Brett has killed herself with aspirins.'

★ ★ ★

Hugh went into the office. It was dusk.

'What the hell's happened out there? An orgy?'

'A few friends called to celebrate the second coming,' Ian said, shifting his feet on the desk. 'I'm tired of the subject. Do you know that crafty little bugger's actually contacted Snark?'

'Bobby? He got through to it?'

'He seems to know what the damn thing thinks about. He's got it coming back.'

'Coming back where?'

'Back to the moon orbit. It'll take days. But how does he do it?'

'He's a very special boy,' Hugh said slowly. 'Very.'

Ian sat up in his chair. 'What do you mean?'

'I mean he's a genius.'

'Is that all?'

'What else?'

'Don't ask me. I'm just the mechanic. Any news?'

'I was here three hours ago. Forgotten?'

'It's slipped my mind. In fact, my mind is slipping. I wish it would slip away. I don't really want to meet my Maker. He's only going to criticize. Not that I'd hear. All those heads, all those mouths in those heads, all multiplied by seventy thousand and all bawling the praises of the Lord. Give me Valhalla and I'll ride into hell on a Rolls bonnet.'

'You're squiffed. Give me one. Large.'

Ian got up to dispense. 'What's happened with you and Bobby?'

'Enigma. I read conundrums in your tone of voice. What do you mean, 'a very special boy'?'

'A prodigy. A genius.'

'Out of this world,' said Ian and passed a filled glass.

'What do *you* mean?' Hugh was startled.

Ian looked at him. 'What do *you* mean?'

Hugh ignored the question. 'He said it will come on the fifteenth. He's worked it out. Don't ask me how.'

'It'll be sooner,' Ian said. 'Astronomical reports show there's an awful lot of abnormal vibrations going on on the outer fringes of the Giant's boot heel.

Waves of the stuff coming our way.'

'I heard.' He drank and changed the subject. 'I went to see my daughters.'

'Just now? You hadn't seen them this afternoon.'

'I've hardly seen them now. Beck said they were dog-tired. Shouted out of the bedroom window. Blew me a kiss. I don't know what they've got in there they don't want me to see.'

'A rhinoceros?' Ian said, and poured more Scotch into his glass. 'You worry too much, Hugh. Everybody needs an early night, now and again. When I have one I sleep for three days. Like my father. But he didn't sleep. Just changed his hot-water bottle. From Flora to Margaret to Fiona — Ah! he lived the good life. Always made me feel deprived.'

'The world is ending, Ian. Can't you feel that?'

'Tomorrow? Why tomorrow I may be myself with Yesterday's Seven Thousand Years. Come, fill the cup . . . '

'It's years since I read Omar.'

'It wasn't Omar really. It was a noble Scot who based his script on a poem by

Omar — Christ! Again!'

He turned and looked out of the window. Once more the universal silence fell over the sky, but only for a few brief seconds. When it passed, Ian looked round from the window.

'Getting shorter,' he said.

'Is that better or worse?'

Ian glanced out of the window. 'Both and either,' he said. 'Whichever is the most hopeful.'

'You'd think there'd have to be noise. Great Sound — '

'A bang; a whimper; instead, an awful nothing. Perhaps that's what we've earned. Who knows?'

'You're tight,' said Hugh. 'I think I'll join you.'

10

The days passed. Silences came by day and by night; some in short periods of a few seconds, some as long as a minute. Because they became more frequent, people began to accept them as a matter of course; a new phase in the world's changing. Fear remained, but so did hope and the two fought seesaw battles with the coming and going of the ominous pauses.

Broadcasts no longer gave time; only a daily approximation to help programme slots, because each global pause meant those seconds gone, but where, nobody knew.

Many years before, Tom Rogers had built a sundial in his garden and set it with all a craftsman's eye for accuracy in siting and compass correctness. Suddenly it became a popular shrine for villagers, because if the sun stopped, so did the sundial, so each day the sundial was always right, and each day the sun shone, hotter and hotter, and the river grew a little smaller and the vegetation drier and began to fade into brown a little faster.

Animals on the farms began to act out of habit. Cows came in to be milked at any time they felt like it. The horses were very restive but then would go suddenly quiet and could not be urged out of it. Birds sang, but stopped suddenly, as if listening. Only the insects marched on in their hidden millions, undisturbed. They were used to disasters, and when flood and fire swept them mostly to death, the rest went on working to build again. The people with dogs knew ahead of the next pause, because the dogs sensed the coming and either hid or stayed unusually close to their owners. Jeff Wise at the pub always knew because Flag came to him and whined a little. Maud Wise began to want to shoot it, as if the coming of the world's end was the dog's fault. She was getting too fretful, no matter what Jeff did to calm her. Sometimes he got so fed up with home life he wished the bloody world would end; then almost fell on his knees to pray that it wouldn't.

On the 10 July, the dark man came to the cottage by the river. Bet was on the launching ramp, looking back at the closed doors of the boat-building shed. She started when she saw him. He came on to the ramp by her.

'I thought you should know, your friend is back in town. Where's the boy?'

'At school. Do you mean that wretched man is here *again*?'

'I saw him not an hour ago. Can't you find somewhere for Bobby to go? Not school.'

'Yes.' She looked at him, then away to the river. 'I'll do that. Thank you for coming.'

'That's all right. I told you — I'm on your side. I can tell you he won't be wanting Bobby till tomorrow. It might be a good idea to get the boy away early morning. Very early. OK?'

'I'm so grateful. But why do they . . . ? It's a sort of persecution.'

He turned away as if about to go, then turned back.

'They're not quite that bad, Mrs Hicks.

But you know who Bobby really is. It's never happened before, as far as anyone knows, and that's the reason Intelligence wants to know.'

'Why wait till the morning?'

'If they see or hear he's about here, they won't worry. If they don't, they will. It's a mentality you have to get used to. It watches abnormality. That is why you can hide almost any evil thing by appearing normal.'

'How did you get into it?'

'As the divorced lady said to her disappointed mother: 'I thought I would like it.'' He turned and walked a few paces away, then looked back. 'If you think I might help, don't hesitate, will you?'

'Thank you. I won't.'

She watched him take his jacket off before he walked on. It was a wonder he could wear it at all in the heat. She dabbed her face with a small handkerchief.

★　★　★

Jeff Wise leant against the pub wall, his legs thrust out from the oak bench.

'Feels the end of the world'll be by boilin',' he said, wiping his face with a bar towel.

'Where's everybody got this idea it's the end of the world?' said the postman.

Drinkers, standing about the dusty yard, began to wonder.

'I dunno where it started,' Jeff said, 'but it's the sort of idea folks like. Exciting. Like a horror picture. Ah well.' He dragged himself up. 'Better get back behind bars before I get bawled at.'

He went inside.

★ ★ ★

'What do you want all those batteries for?' Hugh said. 'Even my chief engineer got shirty about your order.'

'If the world is to end, the mains will be cut out, but a few batteries can help us get in touch with anybody else who might be left.'

'Anybody else?' said Hugh with sarcasm. 'What makes you think you'll survive?'

'Everybody does. There's a religion

which teaches, 'It can't happen to me.' It's the most popular of all.'

'If it gets any hotter I'm not sure I want to stay,' Hugh said. 'The world's spinning a bit off balance. That's what-causing the hiccups. Probably causing the heat, too.'

'Everything is now truly offbeat, off its centre. If it gets worse, we've had it. But you know the mighty midget has the idea we could restore balance by hitting the moon? Did he tell you?'

'Yes. It's a very long shot.'

'So is the fact that we exist at all. Consider that.'

'I had a degree in crackpotism. As I say it's a long shot because if you cut a tiny bit off the moon it *might* affect the balance there, and the gravitational pull *might* steady us, and all would be fairly safe, perhaps, but that can't happen till the Earth's chucked us off, so what's the point? As we sail off beyond the stars into the *ewigkeit* do we shout, 'Oh thank God, the Earth's all right! There's nothing on it, but it's all right.'' He shrugged.

'Nobody's been chucked off it yet, and according to the theories, we all should have been. Nobody's explained that yet. Is it possible great daddy Newton led us up the garden path somewhere?'

'No. But with a shake-out in the universe going on, our natural laws might be upset somehow. That will take time to find out.'

'Before St Swithin's Day?'

'Do you believe everything that boy says?'

'He's getting outside information. Put it like that.'

'The aliens' planet was destroyed, wherever it was, but it seems to have been in the middle of this sidereal tempest. They say we're out of it and they may be in a position to know that. All the same, they can be wrong.'

'Funny how you accept the existence of these extra-terrestrial beings, Hugh.'

'We've got bloody good reason to, haven't we, Ian?'

'Roz might have told a little fib.'

'She has no reason to at this stage. And the stories go back a long time before Roz. They go back to where Bet was conceived. Fairies in the woods. There's always been a legend about strangers in Bell Wood. Bell Wood is on a cross-road of ley lines. It's the site of ancient stone rings, power rings. You know one or two stones are still there now, besides the remains of the temple. They are centres of abnormal magnetic activity, and such could be used as navigational points or beacons, and all evidence shows they have been. I don't know the secret of that damn place by the river but it's there, and if we survive, then one day we shall all have to believe it.'

Ian sat back in his chair. 'It's the heat,' he said. 'Bloody terrible.'

★   ★   ★

'I've rung Auntie Becky. You can go over at six in the morning. The door won't be locked. You'll be all right darling. It's just for tomorrow till the man's gone.'

He sat at the table, eating biscuits and watching her with big eyes.

'He won't have time,' he said.

She stared at him, then turned away with a shrug of impatience.

'Oh, don't be silly. Nobody *knows*,' he said.

He ate another biscuit and watched the open door as if someone might come in from outside.

★ ★ ★

'If it does come, Clara, do you want to be with me?'

She looked up from jotting in a diary. He was putting on his collar to go out to one more meeting. She dropped her pen, sat still for a while, then got up.

'Yes, darling. Yes I do — please.' She began to cry and went into his arms. 'I do. I'm sorry. Oh, Jim!'

★ ★ ★

At 4 a.m. on 14 July, Miss Wainwright rang the bell at the vicarage. She hugged the handle of a holdall across her belly and seemed almost on the point of crying for the door to be answered.

Jim answered, wearing his dressing-gown.

239

'Ethel! What's happened?'

'I'm sorry.' She was breathless as if she had been running . . . 'I wish to resign as secretary to the Parish Council. I cannot keep on any longer. I have here the minute-book, accounts, records . . . ' She ran out of breath.

'My dear Ethel, come in and sit down — '

'No. I cannot continue any longer. Please take these. Everything is there — '

'Ethel, please pull yourself together! There is nothing that will happen to you alone. We must face together these — '

'I am not concerned with that! I am not frightened of my life ending. I shall be grateful when it is over. I have had a hell of conscience and suffering for half my life and — and . . . ' She shuddered, dropped the holdall on the step, turned and walked as fast as she could go down the path to the gate.

'Who on earth is it at this time?' Clara called from the stairs.

'Ethel Wainwright. I think she's ill. I'd better get dressed.'

'She's just breaking up,' Clara said and

sat down on the stairs. 'It'll happen, you know. It's bound to. There isn't anything you can do about it, Jim dear. Just nothing. There will be several before we know — one way or the other. I'll make some tea. It's no good going back to bed now.'

Miss Wainwright went back to her little house and shut herself inside. She got down the collection of little bottles gathered for her complaints over recent years, during which she had pleaded for sleep. She had Mogadon, Pyromethazine and others, but the tiny ones were easiest to swallow when one had to take such a lot.

But first she must clean the house right through.

★   ★   ★

The postman ran into the bar.

'Miss Wainwright's tried to kill herself. Sleeping-tablets. Ring the doc — quick!

Jeff dialled, then realized what he was doing. 'What the hell is this you want? The bloody world's going to end tomorrow . . . Hallo? Doctor Hays? Oh

241

yes, It's rather serious, I'm afraid . . . '

Maud Wise came out of the kitchen.

'I'll go and stay with her till he comes,' she said. 'Poor soul. I had an idea something was wrong there.'

Two hours before the postman called on Miss Wainwright, Bobby Miller left Bet to go to his aunts at Old Will's Cottage. He had his pyjamas and toothbrush and a box of chocolates for them.

He left at six-five. At six-thirty-two by the sun on the dial he came back.

'What's the matter? They said the door would be open.'

'I can't go there, Liz,' he said. 'There's two of them. Up in the bedrooms.'

'What do you mean?'

'I heard them. And Auntie Becky. I heard them up there.'

'What about Ruth?'

'She came on to the stairs. I just said, 'Here's some chocolates for you,' and ran out. I can't go there.'

Bet looked away along the garden path. The new roses were browning at the edges. They'd be dropping before they opened fully.

'Why are you afraid of them?'

There was a pause before he answered, 'I don't know. I can't explain it.'

She felt heavy and tired and sat down on the seat by the sundial.

'But they're the ones who know what is happening, when it will happen. They've told you all about it. They've tried to help, why are you afraid?'

'They want to come here. They want me to help them come here.'

'But they truly have nowhere to go. You told me that.'

'If they come here, they will swallow us. I know that too, Liz. They know so much more than we know. They would be more powerful. Perhaps we wouldn't exist any more if they came.'

'But they are here, Bobby. They are here now!'

'Only ones and twos. To bring the others in they would need a clear field. We could not be here if they came, but they won't try and come till afterwards.'

'But why are you frightened of the few already here?'

243

He said nothing, then sat down beside her.

'I'm the bridge, you see. They depend on me, Liz. They need me to make it a success . . .'

He stopped. So did the world. They sat in the awful silence, waiting.

It was the first hiatus where the awfulness came second to her fear for the boy. She did not know then which to fear most: the man from the laboratories or the people all around that she couldn't see.

He took her hand and held it tight.

'You'll save me, Liz.'

'You'll have to tell me how, darling. I don't know enough to do it alone.'

⋆ ⋆ ⋆

'Anybody'd think the world won't end on Thursday.'

'Do you believe it will, Fred Gage?'

'I don't know. I suppose I don't know what it ought to feel like. No, I suppose I don't believe it. I suppose I believe the waters might burst asunder and the skies split into four and the earth sink down to nothing and all that, but sure enough, beyond all the fire and flood and death and disaster, that bloody letter from the bank will come on Friday.'

'You're a proper fatalist,' said Jeff Wise. 'Gilt-edged.'

⋆ ⋆ ⋆

Mr Barnes turned up at Court with his fellow magistrates.

'I'm a little troubled,' said Mrs Garrick. 'If there is anything in this talk, what is the point of giving a man three months in prison?'

'Angie, we must proceed as if God has provided us with all the future we may need.'

'He probably will, at that,' said Mr Barnes, and felt a chill pixie run laughing through his stomach.

⋆ ⋆ ⋆

'Bobby has not been well,' Bet said. 'I've sent him away for a rest in different surroundings. He will be back on Friday.'

'The sixteenth,' said the fair man. 'May I call again then?'

'You know you will,' said Bet, and really expected there would be one more 16 July.

He bowed his head and left the cottage.

★ ★ ★

Jim took Miss Wainwright to the doctor's.

'I've arranged for her to go into a nursing home for a rest and observation,' he told the vicar. 'She can't be left at home by herself in her state.'

'Of course,' said Jim, and felt a weight lift from his mind.

It was all unreal. It was hardly surprising Miss Wainwright should have broken down under the strangeness in the air of these days.

As he drove home he almost wished there might be some threatening sign of violence to come. These silent hiccups had begun to lose impact because after they had come and gone everything was normal. Thus it was becoming more and more impossible to believe in any such thing as a violent end to the world.

What he did not know then was that the one element which had been disturbed by the pauses was the sea. The tides were starting to vary in their timing and there was an odd, almost oily swell of water which was rising higher, and it was being watched with growing concern by the millions of people who dwelt on the coasts of the world. But that time it was a rising and then falling back as in a normal ebb which calmed most fears with the ebb.

It was a poetic Cornish coastguard who made a report: 'The face of the sea is changing. It has never looked friendly, sometimes evil, sometimes sullen, sometimes placid, and sometimes with the rage of Hell in it, but I never saw it as it is now — starting to *grin*.'

At midday on the 14th news broadcasts said that, due to exceptionally high tides, certain front coastal areas had been put on alert for evacuation if the waters rose more. It was stressed that this was a precaution.

The precaution was also being taken throughout all coastal areas in the world, but in most it was an alert to watchfulness.

Many millions suddenly remembered the age-old fear of the second Flood, and it spread. Pauses were strange and frightening but they brought no visible menace. In the abnormal rising of the oceans, there was.

Quite suddenly the threat of global disaster was real to those near the coasts. Out of reach of the sea, there was a feeling almost of relief.

11

The fifteenth of July dawned the same as all the other days in that long, hot, arid summer. The same mist over the river meadows, the same rich smells of the vegetation gasping the last of the slight night moisture from the swindling water, and the same rapid increase of the night warmth to burning heat.

As if they knew that Rustum Magna was to be one of the last small places to survive, people awoke that morning with the feeling that this was like no other day. The young people did not go to catch the bus out to work and the school bus went away empty.

'Superstition is a wonderful thing,' said Fred Gage, as he drove the empty bus back behind his garage.

At eight, in proof of faith unquenchable, Fred's father, Seth Gage, arrived in the village on his bicycle and rode into the churchyard to wind the clock in the

Norman tower as he had done for forty years, once a week. As he opened the church door a man called out:

'How long d'you think that'll tick for, Gage?'

Suddenly the day felt cold all round. Some people in the street turned and looked the other way. Others looked as if they had suddenly thought of something important. Only two stared in disbelief.

Jim had had twenty people for communion that morning, the highest, by eighteen, since Christmas. Fourteen had stayed on sitting in the church, to wait.

'That's what we'll all be doing,' Jeff Wise said, staring out of the pub window, 'watching, waiting, letting the day roll on, and in the end nothing will happen and so it'll have to be going to happen another day. You see.'

'I wish it wasn't so *hot*,' Maud said.

★ ★ ★

'You turned up,' said Bet, watching him.

He switched off the planer. The

workshop was quiet after the angry whine.

'I had to think,' he said.

'You'll be no good as a partner if you have to go away for four days to think.'

'It wasn't boats I was thinking over.' He was looking down at the planer, then he looked up. 'Why did you laugh?'

'The plane made a funny noise.'

He looked askance at her. 'It made me deaf,' he said.

'I'm sorry.'

'You must be a fool. I'd better get on. Wasted time, those days.'

'This is a funny sort of day to come back, isn't it?'

He looked at the planer again. 'I don't think so. Can't waste time wondering what God might do. And if he does it? Well, it happened before. Floods, earthquakes, Sodom ... He never kills everybody, does he? Let Him sort it out.'

He turned back to his work.

'The glue came,' she said, and felt a curious little excitement.

His face lit up as he turned and looked at her.

'Good,' he said. His smile faded as his gaze intensified. He dropped the planer, then bent down to pick it up. 'Sod it.'

She turned angrily and went to the doors. She stopped on the way out and turned.

'Do you want to talk about the partnership?'

He looked up again, more pleased than over glue.

'Yes, I would.'

'Come to the cottage. I keep the figures there.'

He put the planer on a bench and followed her.

★ ★ ★

The room of the machines was dark by comparison with the white sunlight through the window. The boy glanced at the flickering diodes, then typed some digits on the keyboard and watched the screen in front of him.

Ritchie turned from the radar screens and looked at him.

'Got a signal?' Ritchie said.

'Yes. It's on course. About five o'clock is the ETA, but that's rough now.'

'Suppose nothing happens?'

'You can send it away for a while.'

'Isn't anybody else picking this up?'

'Not the signal. They haven't got the right keying. Is that what you call it?'

'Near enough.' Ritchie turned away and sat on a small table. 'Two nights running I saw some sort of disc on the star screen, right over this village. It was like a shadow. Both times it suddenly shrank and vanished. Is that anything you know about?'

'It's a ship. Landing people.'

'These people of yours?'

'They're not whole people. They land the shadows. They won't be solid until it's safe. That's what they told me.'

'What are they doing?'

'Spying out everything. For when they come. They follow ladies. They made Miss Wainwright ill.'

'How do you know?'

'They went to her house. They went to Mrs Brett's, too.'

'Why didn't you say anything?'

'I was afraid. I'd only tell you, or Uncle Hugh, or Liz. I couldn't tell those men who came. I couldn't tell anybody else.'

Ian watched him.

'Now you know who you are, Bobby, what would you do if they do come?'

Bobby looked at him, then he got up from the chair and tears made his wide stare brighter. He shook his head.

'I belong here!' He pointed to the floor by the door like a baby pointing for something. 'I belong here! Liz won't let me go.' His voice faded and he began to cry silently.

Ian got up and took the boy in his arms.

'Easy now,' he said, and wondered what he was talking about, when over the boys' head he watched the screens which were showing already the beginnings of an upheaval which clearly would not stop before the world of men had been swept away.

A phantom voice from the corner said: ' . . . a compilation of present indications are beginning to show evidences of shock waves crossing the solar system in close

254

proximity to the Earth at speeds of . . . I will check that first . . . '

'I'm all right, Uncle Ian! I'm all right!' Bobby pushed free and went to the door. 'I want to find Liz.' He ran out.

Ritchie watched the window and saw the boy appear on the grass at the left hand side of it. Bobby was running, but not towards Liz's cottage. He ran the opposite way, and ran as if demented.

' . . . and at this rate the main wave will strike Earth at approximately 11.21 present Greenwich Mean Time today. So earlier waves . . . '

'Any news?'

Ian turned as Hugh came in. Ian told him as the bulletin ended.

'The boy was right all along,' Ian said. 'And he's ordering in Snark.'

'Is anybody else on it?'

'No. That was the point of the design, wasn't it?'

'I mean our lot! The military who sent it up.'

'Sod them. The boy's been right when nobody else knew. He has been getting the information from people who *know*.

Let him have Snark, for what the wise men know may put us right if the whole damn ball spins off course. It's a chance — *if* the whole thing does go.'

'You're depending on aliens to get us out of it.'

'They *know*. They're the only ones who do know. They've had it. Their ball was destroyed. These few who survived are just floaters with nowhere to go, but they've had all the experience we've never had. Let's use it.'

'Agreed. But supposing they do steady things down and save a few of mankind, and then they have more in their floating ships than we have left on earth. What happens then?'

'Do you want to live to see what happens? That is the point for decision. You can't say choice, because there is none.' He pointed suddenly. 'Look at that satellite picture. Look at it!'

Hugh looked at the screen. The British Isles and part of Europe was outlined on the glass, but there was a strange whirling circle of green that blotted out Scotland, the western half of Ireland, the north of

France, the Netherlands and a part of Germany. The circle was slowly closing inwards and spreading outwards, blanking out more and more land as the rim swelled.

'That's not cloud!' Hugh said.

'It's water,' Ian said. 'The sea. It's starting to spin . . . '

Both men looked at the window. The silence was on again. Hugh turned, opened the door and went out through the barn to the open air. Ian came out behind him, then nothing moved anywhere. The world had stopped.

But the silence was not quite as before. There seemed to be a steady, hushing sound, very far away; the shadow of a sound coming from the sky.

'Can you hear that?'

'Yes.'

'What is it?'

Ian listened. 'It's the sea,' he said. 'That's the only thing on earth that never stops.'

The silence held, longer and longer. The constant sound of the far-off sky seemed a part of the silence. Then, slowly at first, the light changed. The sky, blue for so many days, began to turn gold and then copper in colour. The sun began to turn a deeper red as if some sidereal mist faded across it. And in the strange silence, the sun began to move, slowly but definitely towards the south. The two men dropped to all fours, as if to cling to the ground for fear of being thrown off into nothing. But there was no movement in the earth; the sun alone moved, down the sky to the south. And as it sank a great scimitar shape of blackness rose up across the sky from the north; a great shadow of the falling sun.

The sun vanished below the southern horizon, and the racing bow of night chased down the sky in pursuit. The mighty drama swept across the heaven in silence until somewhere in the vast sky of sparkling stars above there sounded a solitary howling, a great cry of an unknown astral body falling alone through the sparkling void to eternity, and then it was gone.

They heard a sound rising all around, the roar of a spinning sea whirling across the land, phosphorescent under the new night of stars that had never been seen above that land before.

The tempest had passed. The Earth was falling, taking all its life still hugging to its surface as it oscillated off an axis that had never been secure.

And through the changing pattern of the stars a single silver mite noses in towards its target, following wherever it moved in the shifting bowl of sidereal storm. It struck, like a pin into the surface of a mountain, and created a puff and a drifting of piling sands across the pocked landscape of the satellite.

Immeasurable time passed and then the perpetual darkness began to change into grey and into a day of great piling cloud masses which came with rising winds, like new breath roaring out again, and so rain.

It was the rain that brought life back to the village; a place now an island in a receding sea, a vale in a plateau with its guardian hills around, the centre of the gigantic spin of devastation, the centre of the spinning disc that does not move.

★ ★ ★

When the men got up from the grass with limbs that needed to be forced, they went back to the aged barn. It was silent inside but now and again an agitated tile high above slid away down over the others and dropped to the ground outside.

The cathode ray screens in the dark room still shone, but from the batteries. There was no picture from a satellite, for that too had flown away into nowhere. The radar showed only sea; endless, restless sea, digesting the remains of a world.

'We must see who's left.'

'What do we do then?'

'Build again. What else was there ever for us to do?'

★ ★ ★

But there was no rebuilding for a while, nor travel as the sea remained circling the hills round the vale of Rustum.

They were days of giant storms and torrential rains. The rain streamed off the

260

dried meadows and filled the withered stream, and an angry flood of frothing waters surged round the bend in Bell Wood and roared down the gentle fall through the gap in the hills and into the surly waters to disturb the wreck-strewn patterns on the sullen surface. At times lightning was so continuous it looked as if the sunken power grid was trying to assert its power once more. The days were much longer than the old ones, and the continuing warfare of the storms made them seem longer still.

And then one night, the storms fled down the sky and the surrounding sea abated in its fury and continued in that continuous ebbing which had saved Rustum drowning in the flood of its own river.

* * *

The morning came in stillness, and a great blue sky, dappled with little island clouds painted pink on their bellies was magically still in the lucid dawnlight.

And still and silent in the sky, floated

261

several great shining black discs, a series of plates spun in by an unseen giant from the south. There was no sound from them, nor any movement. On the ground some birds sang in Bell Wood.

'They've come,' Hugh said.

'I am a wee newt at the bottom of a still pond, looking up at the water lilies. Suddenly I know I'm not going to be a frog.'

'No,' said the woman. 'They are not a bad people. Remember. *I know.*'

We do hope that you have enjoyed reading this large print book.

Did you know that all of our titles are available for purchase?

We publish a wide range of high quality large print books including:
Romances, Mysteries, Classics
General Fiction
Non Fiction and Westerns

Special interest titles available in large print are:
The Little Oxford Dictionary
Music Book, Song Book
Hymn Book, Service Book

Also available from us courtesy of Oxford University Press:
Young Readers' Dictionary
(large print edition)
Young Readers' Thesaurus
(large print edition)

For further information or a free brochure, please contact us at:
Ulverscroft Large Print Books Ltd.,
The Green, Bradgate Road, Anstey,
Leicester, LE7 7FU, England.
Tel: (00 44) **0116 236 4325**
Fax: (00 44) **0116 234 0205**

DEATH CALLED AT NIGHT

R. A. Bennett

Jimmy Ellis believes his parents have died in a car crash when as a young boy he is taken to live with relatives in Australia. The years pass happily, then the nightmare comes. Terrifying images flit through his mind in the dark — all through the eyes of a child, a witness to grisly events seventeen years before. He begins to delve into the past, and soon he finds himself on the trail of a double murderer — a murderer who is prepared to kill again.

THE DEAD TALE-TELLERS

John Newton Chance

Jonathan Blake always kept appointments. He had kept many, in all sorts of places, at all sorts of times, but never one like that one he kept in the house in the woods in the fading light of an October day. It seemed a perfect, peaceful place to visit and perhaps take tea and muffins round the fire. But at this appointment his footsteps dragged, for he knew that inside the house the men with whom he had that date were already dead . . .

SEA VENGEANCE

Robert Charles

Chief Officer John Steele was disillusioned with his ship; the *Shantung* was the slowest old tramp on the China Seas, and her Captain was another fading relic. The *Shantung* sailed from Saigon, the port of war-torn Vietnam, and was promptly hijacked by the Viet Cong. John Steele, helped by the lovely but unpredictable Evelyn Ryan, gave them a much tougher fight than they had expected, but it was Captain Butcher who exacted a final, terrible vengeance.